LISTEN AND I'LL TELL YOU

LISTEN AND I'LL TELL YOU

EDWARD KOREL

WITH ILLUSTRATIONS BY
QUENTIN BLAKE

J. B. LIPPINCOTT COMPANY
Philadelphia and New York

PART ONE

THE CROWS AND THE OWLS

1

The Quarrel

In the South of India there is a village near which stands a huge banyan tree with countless branches. In this tree lived the Crow-King and his followers. And at the time the story begins everything was in a turmoil. For the Owl-King had declared war on the crows and had sworn to kill as many of them as opportunity allowed. And judging by the number of dead crows to be found lying all over the forest, it seemed that opportunity was in a very generous mood indeed. Only the night before the owl armies had raided the banyan tree, hurled nests to the ground, and killed all the crows they had been able to capture.

This unhappy business had started some time before when it was decided to elect a King of all the Birds. The geese, cranes, doves, swans, partridges, nightingales, peacocks and all the other bird clans held a meeting, and after much discussion decided to elect an owl as King of all the Birds. They were just about to crown him when there was an interruption from someone in the assembly.

'Hear me!' cawed the piercing voice of a crow. 'Listen to me before it's too late.'

All was suddenly quiet.

'It would be a terrible mistake to elect this creature as our King.' There were angry screechings and flutterings at these words.

'The owl is said to be the wisest of birds,' continued the crow undisturbed. 'But is he?'

'He isn't an interfering busybody like some people,' cackled a goose pointedly.

'He doesn't talk too much either,' sneered a crane.

'And he listens to what other people say,' declared a partridge.

'Exactly,' replied the crow, ignoring their rude remarks. 'He listens to what we say and never utters a word. But the reason's quite simple. He's silent because he's blind, and doesn't know what's going on around him. But what's the good of a blind leader?'

At this there was renewed chattering among the birds. And one or two of them who had been afraid to say anything before raised a small cheer. Encouraged by this the crow continued: 'What we want is a leader who is clever at all times, someone who uses all his five wits. We want someone like——' He hesitated and smiled to himself, 'like the monkey who outwitted the crocodile.'

'A monkey outwit a crocodile?' said a peacock laughing. 'How did he do that?'

'Listen and I'll tell you,' said the crow.

THE MONKEY AND THE CROCODILE

Once there was a monkey who lived in the branches of a rose-apple tree beside a river. One day a crocodile climbed on to the bank to sun himself and Monkey, being a friendly soul, offered him one of the red apples to eat. Seeing that he

14

enjoyed it he offered him another, and soon they became the best of friends. Crocodile came daily to visit him and seldom left without a snoutful of apples for his wife.

One day Crocodile got home to find his wife, a nagging quarrelsome woman, in one of her nagging quarrelsome moods.

'And where have you been today?' she demanded as soon as he swam through the door.

'I've been to see my friend Monkey.'

'What, Monkey again? It was Monkey the day before yesterday, Monkey yesterday and now it's Monkey today. I suppose it'll be Monkey tomorrow as well. You don't spend much time at home these days.'

'He's sent you some apples, dear,' said Crocodile patiently.

'Apples indeed!' snorted his wife. Nevertheless she took the fruit. And it was obvious from the way she ran her tongue round her teeth when she had finished that she had enjoyed them.

'I've been thinking,' she said, when all the apples were gone. 'That monkey friend of yours must be very healthy if he lives on fruit like this.'

'He is indeed,' replied her husband.

'And his heart must be good too.'

'There's no doubt about it. The way he swings from tree to tree one would think that——'

'I mean, his heart must be almost pure gold.'

'Indeed it is. He's the kindest, most generous creature I've ever——'

'Fool!' interrupted his wife. 'I mean real gold. They say that good food and healthy exercise turns the heart to gold.'

'Does it?' said Crocodile. 'I didn't know that——'

'Fetch me his heart,' commanded his wife suddenly.

'H-his heart?'

'Yes, I want his heart. If I eat a golden heart I shall never have a day's sickness in my life and shall live for ever.'

Crocodile was horrified. 'I can't kill Monkey!' he protested. 'We're almost brothers.'

'A good husband I've got!' shrieked his wife. 'I suppose my health doesn't matter to you?'

'Of course it does. But there's nothing wrong with it.'

'You think more of your friends than you do of me.'

'It doesn't matter what you say,' said Crocodile quietly. 'I won't kill my friend.'

'So now it doesn't matter what I say,' cried his wife, the tears running down her snout and her tail whirling angrily. 'It never matters what I say. It's always your friends that count; it's always someone else. First it was that hideous Alligator person, then that Buffalo creature who was always stirring up the water, and now it's . . . it's this Monkey.'

'Don't excite yourself, dear,' pleaded Crocodile. 'You know that I do listen to what you say and that I always——'

'If you really love me you'll fetch me that monkey's heart.'

'But I can't!'

'You don't love me. You've never loved me. I shouldn't have married you. It's your friends you love, not your wife.'

And she shrieked and thrashed about and blamed poor Crocodile for all her unhappiness until at last, in order to quieten her, he promised to bring Monkey home the very next day so that she could eat his heart.

The following afternoon he found Monkey, perched as usual on the branches of the rose-apple tree beside the river. Monkey, delighted to see him, produced a heap of freshly picked apples.

'Thank you,' said Crocodile. 'Er—you know, Monkey,' he

said, 'it's been nearly six months since we first met, hasn't it?'

'Just about,' agreed Monkey.

'And I must have eaten nearly a hundred meals with you?'

'I suppose you have.'

'And yet, you've never once been to my house for a meal. It isn't right. My wife was saying only last night that you ought to come and eat with us.'

'But how can I do that?' asked Monkey. 'I live on land and you in the water. I'd drown in your house.'

'No, you wouldn't,' replied his friend. 'You see, we live on a sand bank half in the water and half out of it. On warm days we lie in the sun on the top floor. We could have a meal there.'

'In that case I'd be delighted to accept your invitation,' said Monkey politely. 'I've got no engagements this evening.'

'Good, then you can come back with me. Er—my wife would like nothing better,' added Crocodile slyly.

Later that day, Crocodile, with Monkey on his back, swam home for an evening meal. But it was Monkey who was to be the meal. Monkey was chatting happily. He praised Crocodile on his careful swimming, admired the water lilies and flowering shrubs beside the river, enjoyed the warmth of the water, and was the best of travelling companions. But all this only made Crocodile feel miserable. He was a traitor! Poor trusting Monkey, Monkey who had always made him so welcome, Monkey who had entertained him for hours with stories of the forest, Monkey who was delighted to come to his house and meet his wife——

At last he could stand it no longer. 'Monkey, old chap,' he called suddenly.

'Yes, what is it?'

'Monkey, I—I've got a confession to make, a terrible

confession. I—I'm not taking you home as a guest.'

'But didn't your wife invite me?'

'She invited you all right, but not for the reason you think. My wife is a—a rather headstrong woman.'

'But what's wrong with that? An intelligent woman makes an excellent companion.'

'I said "headstrong", not intelligent,' corrected Crocodile.

'I see.'

'And very often she gets strange ideas into her head.'

'Does she?'

'Yes. At the moment she's taken it into her head that because you live on those beautiful apples your heart must be pure gold.'

'That's very kind of——'

'And she's asked me to take you home so that she can——'

'Make interesting conversation with me?'

'Eat your heart and live for ever.'

'I see.'

'I—I'm awfully sorry, but there's no stopping her once she gets these ideas into her head.'

Monkey did some quick thinking, but the only expression on his face was that of disappointment.

'Tut! Tut!' he said, shaking his head as if disappointed.

'I knew it would come as a shock to you,' Crocodile remarked sadly.

'It's not that. I—I'm afraid I'm going to have to disappoint you. I'm sorry to say I haven't brought it along with me.'

'What, you haven't got your heart with you?'

'No, it's much too valuable to carry about.'

'But how do you manage to——'

'Oh, I've got an ordinary one for everyday use. I leave the golden one hidden safely in the rose-apple tree.'

'What shall I do?' asked Crocodile. 'I daren't go home without it. My wife'll——'

'Don't worry, old friend,' replied Monkey consolingly, 'I know how you feel. And because of our great friendship, I'll make her a present of the golden heart.'

'Oh, would you?' Crocodile exclaimed gratefully.

'It's not much use to me, and it's a big responsibility having an expensive thing like that to look after. Take me back to the tree and I'll get it immediately.'

'Thank you! Thank you!' said Crocodile. And he turned round and took Monkey back to his house.

But no sooner had they reached the shore than Monkey scrambled speedily up into the tree. And that was the last poor, foolish, hen-pecked Crocodile ever saw of him.

'That's the kind of leader we want, a quick-witted, sensible creature, not a blind, foolish old mouse-chaser,' added the crow when his story was finished.

At this the birds began once more to argue amongst themselves, some insisting still that the owl was the best choice, others that a blind king was worse than no king at all. And at nightfall they were still arguing. One after the other they flew away to their nests until only the owl, a few bats and a nightingale were left. And the nightingale scurried quickly away before the owl was able to focus his attention on her.

The next day at dawn the birds reassembled to discuss the coronation of the owl. Support for the crow was increasing, especially among the smaller birds who feared the owl.

'Friends,' he cawed, 'I'm pleased that some of you have been thinking about my words. Here is another thought for you.' He paused and waited for silence before continuing. 'We are all agreed that our King must be a wise, unbiased judge, are we not?'

Everyone nodded.

'But how can we be sure that the owl can be that? How can we be sure that he won't just be another "hermit cat"?'

'A hermit cat?' asked a pigeon. 'What did he do?'

Once there was a partridge who lived very comfortably in a hole on some rough ground not very far from the River Jumna. Now it happened that one year there were more hunters about than usual and for the sake of his health Partridge decided to fly to another part of the country and stay with relatives. But no sooner had he gone than a rabbit from a near-by copse moved into his home. And when Partridge returned he found his comfortable, leaf-lined burrow occupied by a large brown and white rabbit, his buxom blue-grey wife, and a number of tiny brown, white, blue and grey baby rabbits with soft twitching noses and ears at different angles.

'What are you doing in my home?' Partridge demanded angrily.

'I beg your pardon?' said Rabbit civilly.

'I said, what are you doing in my home?'

'It's not your home, it's my home.'

'It's not!' insisted Partridge, more angry still. 'You waited till I went away and then stole my home. You're a thief—a house thief! That's what you are!'

'My dear friend,' replied Rabbit good-humouredly. 'Don't excite yourself. The matter's really quite simple. You abandoned your home and I took it over. You can't call me a thief if I pick up something that you throw away.'

'But I didn't throw my home away. I only went to stay with relatives until the hunters had gone.'

'How was I to know that you'd be back?' asked Rabbit. 'You didn't leave any message. Anyway, I've worked very hard making this hole larger for my wife and family. We've been here three months already and we're not leaving it now.'

'But it's my home!' persisted Partridge. 'I've lived here all my life. My father lived here before me, and his father before him.'

'Then you shouldn't have left it.'

'But I didn't leave it!'

'You did!'

'I didn't!'

'Yes, you did! Otherwise I wouldn't be here now.'

And so the two went on, each arguing that the place was his, and neither willing to give way to the other. At last Rabbit, still the calmer of the two, said, 'I see we're getting nowhere. Let's take the matter to law and decide which of us is the rightful owner of the property. There's a hermit cat living on the river bank. He's a very serious, religious person, and well qualified to judge this case.'

'A cat?' queried Partridge astonished. 'You and I can't trust a cat, religious or otherwise.'

'Ah, but this is a special cat. You've only to hear him speak to realize that.'

And so Rabbit and Partridge went together to the hermitage to hear the judgment of the wise cat.

Now this so-called "hermit cat" was really no more religious than any other cat, but pretended to be so to save himself the bother of hunting for his food. And very few of the small, appetizing creatures who went to him for advice were ever seen or heard of again. For the benefit of visitors who inquired about the large number of bones around the place, he explained that they were the relics of saints. He saw Rabbit and Partridge coming in the distance. Quickly sitting himself down on the ground he cupped his chin in his paw, and assumed a serious look on his face as if the deepest of deep problems were occupying his mind. In actual fact he was wondering whether to have Rabbit for lunch and save Partridge for supper, or vice-versa.

'Er—excuse me,' called Rabbit from a distance. Neither he nor Partridge was brave enough to go too near.

But Cat pretended not to hear.

'Er—excuse me,' called Rabbit again.

'Eh? What's that? What? Ah, yes,' answered Cat finally. 'I'm sorry I didn't hear you. I was er—er thinking.'

'What about?' asked Rabbit.

'Ah me,' sighed Cat. 'I'm afraid my thoughts weren't very happy ones. And anyway, I don't expect they'd interest you.'

'Yes, they would,' replied Rabbit, who liked nothing better than to sit himself on a comfortable heap of dried leaves and think about things.

'Come a little closer then and I'll tell you. It's difficult to discuss serious things at the top of one's voice.'

The animals came closer.

'I was thinking about the cruelty of the world,' began Cat. He shook his head sadly and lifted his eyes pitifully towards heaven.

'It's terrible to think how animals hunt and kill each other. And why do they do it? Why, for food! It's too horrible to think about. Even cats kill mice and birds and other harmless creatures. And what do they do with them? They eat them. It's horrible, horrible.'

'Er—what do you eat?' asked Partridge.

'Me?' replied Cat. 'Why, I eat—er grass shoots, chestnuts—things like that. Now and again I might have a dish of baked acorns. Nothing more. No meat! No. Not meat or game! Horrible stuff! It makes me feel queer to think of it.'

'I'm very pleased to hear it,' said Partridge. 'I thought that maybe you——'

'No! Never! What a thought! I'm hurt. I'll have to shut my eyes for a minute. I feel quite faint.'

'Oh, I'm very sorry,' cried Partridge, 'I didn't mean to——'

'Don't give it another thought,' replied Cat, recovering very quickly from his sudden fit and smiling forgivingly at his visitors. 'But what can I do for you?'

'I want justice,' said Partridge. 'I left my home for a little while when the hunters were about, and when I came back this rabbit, his wife and a huge family of children had moved in. Now is it——'

'He moved out, so I moved in,' interrupted Rabbit. 'If he wanted his home he shouldn't have left——'

'But I didn't leave it,' cried Partridge.

'Yes, you did! Otherwise I shouldn't have moved in in the first place.'

'But I intended to come back.'

'How was I to know that?'

'You might have used your common sense.'

'Common sense? If you'd have had any common sense you wouldn't have——'

'Stop it! Stop it!' called Cat in a pained voice. 'All this is most distressing. How can I be expected to give judgment with all this shouting going on? I'll have to take down your evidence privately. Come into my cave one at a time and

24

I'll examine your arguments. It's too bad that you should harbour such angry thoughts about each other.' He turned to Partridge. 'As you say the property used to belong to you, I'd better hear your evidence first.' And forgetting his earlier fears, poor Partridge walked into the cave with Cat.

Rabbit who was waiting outside wished to hear the evidence Partridge was giving Cat and crept over to the mouth of the cave to listen. At first he heard Partridge repeat his argument about the place belonging to his father and his grandfather. But suddenly the talking stopped. For a moment there was silence. Then he heard Partridge talking very quickly and in a very frightened voice. 'Stop! What are you doing? No! Don't come near me! No! Don't! I thought you said you only ate grass shoots and—and chestnuts. No! Stop! Oh——' Then all was silent.

Rabbit had heard enough of the kind of justice dispensed by Cat. And before he could be invited to enter the witness box, or whatever it was that Cat called his pantry, he bounded away towards the long grass and the safety of his home. For now it was his home. Poor Partridge was never to return to claim it. But he would have liked the matter to have been settled in a rather different way.

The assembly were quiet and thoughtful as they listened to this tale. There were a great many head-shakings and shoulder shruggings, and one by one the birds returned to their nests, leaving the owl uncrowned and very angry indeed at the interference of the crow. And from that day to this the owls and crows have been the bitterest of enemies, although it was the crows who suffered most. For the fiercer owls repeatedly attacked their headquarters at night and killed as many of them as they could lay their claws on.

One morning the Crow King called together his followers. 'Things are becoming desperate,' he announced. 'Last night, as you all know, the owls again attacked our city and killed many of our people. Maybe they will come again tonight, tomorrow night or the night after. What are we to do?'

There was silence. Everyone knew the position to be hopeless.

'There are few paths open to us,' continued the King. 'There is attack. But that would be foolish. For they are much stronger than we are. Or we could surrender. But that would be suicide. They would spare none of our lives.'

'Could we not make a peace treaty with them?' someone asked.

'No, they have sworn to kill us and would never agree to let us live peacefully.'

'Could we not form an alliance with another clan?'

'Who?' asked the King. 'The owls can see in the dark and are night fighters. No one would dare join us in attacking them. No! It looks as if——' He paused sadly and looked gloomily at the assembly. 'It looks as if we'll have to abandon our city and scatter into the forest. There's no alternative. If we stay here we'll die. If we leave our homes, although we'll have to be away from our relatives and friends for some time, perhaps one day we will all——'

'Your Majesty!' A loud voice interrupted these gloomy words.

'What is it, White Wings?'

White Wings was one of the King's most important advisers. He had listened gravely to all that had been said before offering his own advice. He was a tall crow, bigger than most of his fellows. He had been given this curious name because of the patches of white under both his wings.

'Your Majesty has forgotten an important alternative,' he said slowly.

'And what's that?'

'Most of the great victories of the world, Your Majesty, have been won by trickery—and some of the smaller ones too,' he added, smiling to himself.

'Why are you smiling?' asked the King.

'I've reminded myself of the story of the thief's goat, Your Majesty.'

'Can we hear it?' asked the King. 'Perhaps it will make us a little happier.'

THE THIEF'S GOAT

Once there was a thief. He was a huge, ugly, scowling fellow and had bloodshot eyes. Like most thieves he went about his business at night and in the early hours of the morning. And one day just before dawn, he was returning home from a visit to a neighbouring village with a stolen goat on his shoulders, when he was seen by three rogues who prowled about the villages at all hours to see if there was anything worthy of their attention. When they saw the thief returning with his prize they decided upon a plan to save him the trouble of carrying the heavy animal all the way home. One of them stepped on to the path to greet him. The thief was thinking of the big meal and the comfortable bed awaiting him on his return when his thoughts were suddenly interrupted.

'Good morning!'

He looked up to see a stranger smiling cheerfully beside him.

' 'Morning!' he replied sharply, not wishing to get into conversation.

'That's a funny looking dog you've got there,' said the man. The thief stopped.

'Dog!' he began, 'but——'

'Mind you,' interrupted the stranger, 'I suppose you're carrying it home to give it a decent burial, but I'd be more careful what I carried on my shoulders. Apart from fleas, you never know what else——'

'Idiot!' exploded the thief. 'It isn't a dog. If you used your eyes you'd see it was a goat.'

'A goat?' queried the stranger as if surprised. He looked

closely at it. Then he touched it. 'Why yes—of course. But I could have sworn it was a——'

But the thief had continued on his way before he could finish the sentence.

'Fool!' he grunted to himself. 'A dog! Humph! Some people have no more brains than a——'

'Good morning!'

Another traveller had suddenly appeared on the road.

' 'Morning!' grunted the thief.

'You know,' said the stranger, 'I haven't seen such a fine sheep for a long time. It's not often that you get one that's so——'

'Sheep——' began the thief.

'Mind, you want to be careful. There's a lot of disease about nowadays and people do say that it comes from animals. But I suppose this one died from——'

'Are you mad?' cried the thief. 'It's not a sheep. Look carefully, clown, and you'll see it's a goat.'

'A goat? Are you sure? Why, bless my soul, so it is! Do you know, it looked exactly like a sheep when I saw you walking along with it on your——'

But the thief had continued on his way.

'Another lunatic,' he growled to himself. 'This place is full of them. The first one said it was a dog—the second a sheep—— Humph! Mad! Mad!' Nevertheless he stopped, put the animal on the ground and examined it. 'Of course it's a goat!' He scratched his head. 'I wonder what made the second fellow think it was a sheep. And what about the first one——?' Slowly he picked the goat up and walked on. 'Course it's a goat,' he said once more glancing at it. 'What I can't understand is how anyone could have——'

'Good morning!' Yet another traveller.

'Good morning,' repeated the man bowing politely.

''Morning!' snorted the thief. 'Er—I'm in a hurry, I——'

'I had to stop to say how much I admired your strength,' interrupted the man.

'Thanks!' grunted the thief. 'Now I'd better be getting——'

'It isn't every man who can carry a donkey so easily.'

The thief looked up quickly. 'A donkey——?'

'A big animal too. Those ears! They're almost as big as its head. If I'm any judge of animals, I'd say it was the largest donkey in the whole of the——'

'Stop!' shrieked the thief, hurling the animal to the ground. 'Stop! I can't stand it! It's not a donkey, dolt! Look!'

'My good fellow,' said the man astonished. 'Are you feeling all right? You seem to be terribly upset. Is there something?'

'I'm not upset,' cried the thief.

'I'm pleased to hear it. I thought perhaps, that the weight of the donkey had——'

'It's not a donkey. It's a—a sheep. No! It's not a sheep. It's a—a——'

'Now, now,' said the man comfortingly. 'Just you rest a moment and everything'll be all right. Of course, it's just as you say. Er—what did you say it was?'

'A dog. No! Not a dog! It's a—a g-goat,' he sobbed.

'Of course, of course. That's quite right. It's a g-goat, isn't it?' he said soothingly. 'Now just try to rest for a few moments and you'll soon feel much better. These morning mists sometimes have a strange effect upon people.'

'M-maybe it's that,' agreed the thief.

'It's only just a turn. You'll feel better in a moment.' He bent down to pick up the animal. 'Let me help you. I'll just put the donkey back on your shoulder and——'

'No! No!' shrieked the thief, his face anguished and his

30

body trembling. 'Keep it! I don't want it! I don't ever want to see it again!'

And scorning any more help he brushed madly past the traveller and hurried down the road leaving the prize goat for anyone who wanted it.

The Crow King smiled when he heard the story, but his smile lasted only a short while.

'Unfortunately,' he said, 'our enemies the owls are not as foolish as that thief.'

'Both fools and wise men may be tricked, Your Majesty,' replied White Wings, 'although the foolish make the easiest victims. Has Your Majesty ever heard of the Donkey who was an ass?'

'No,' the King replied. 'What was that all about?'

THE DONKEY WHO WAS AN ASS

One day a lion who lived in the forest in the South was foolish enough to get into a fight with a great bull elephant, and although it was the elephant who got the worst of it, he himself was so badly hurt that it was many days before he was able to go hunting again. He sat mournfully on the floor of his den groaning and licking his wounds.

Now this lion had a servant, a fox who, willing as he was to share his master's good fortune and food, was not so willing to share his misfortune and starve. And as one hungry day followed the next, and the lion showed no signs of improving, he decided at last to take matters into his own hands.

'Master,' he said, 'we can't go on like this. We—er—I mean you haven't had a good meal in a fortnight.'

'I know,' replied the lion, 'but what can I do? I can't go

hunting in my present state. I'd fall prey myself to any strong animal.'

'I've thought of that,' replied Fox. 'The best thing we can do is this. I'll go out and fetch an animal for you to kill.'

'But what animal would be foolish enough to walk into a lion's den?' asked his master.

'Don't you worry, I'll find one,' said Fox, and with a saucy tilt of his head and a swish of his tail, he left the cave.

'He won't be back very soon,' the lion said to himself when Fox had gone. 'Now maybe I can have some peace.'

Fox had not gone very far when he reached the outskirts of a village. And there in the middle of a field overgrown with weeds and prickly grass, he saw a very unhappy-looking donkey. 'Good morning,' he said politely.

The donkey looked up sadly and returned the greeting.

'If you'll excuse my saying so,' said Fox, 'I don't think very much of this grass you're eating.'

'Neither do I,' replied Donkey gloomily. 'But it's all there is to eat. My master's too mean to hire a piece of grazing land.'

Fox looked back over his shoulder towards the forest.

'What a difference,' he murmured half to himself and half aloud. 'What a difference.'

'What is?' asked Donkey.

'Why, the difference between this dusty grass and the emerald turf in the forest where I live. Er—perhaps you'd like to come and have some of that. There's more than enough for everybody.'

'But I can't go into the forest,' protested Donkey. 'It's much too dangerous a place for us village beasts.'

'Don't be silly. You don't imagine that I'd live in a place where there was any danger. I'm not a fighter.'

'Still,' replied Donkey, 'you're much cleverer than I am. You've got a good brain and can keep out of trouble, whereas I'm such a fool that I——'

'Oh well, I suppose I'd better tell you the truth,' interrupted Fox suddenly.

'The truth? What about?'

Fox looked first one way, then the other. Then he turned to Donkey and gave him a knowing wink. 'There's—er— there's a reason I want you to come into the forest,' he confessed. 'You see——' He broke off. 'You won't tell anyone about this, will you?'

'No.'

'Well there's—there's a very pretty she-donkey living in a cave not far away. And she's—she's looking—for a husband.' At these words Donkey forgot that he was unhappy, forgot the dusty grass he was eating, in fact, he forgot to think at all.

'Did you say a—a she-donkey, a—a pretty one?'

Fox nodded.

'But what's she doing in the forest?'

'She's run away from a farmer who ill-treated her. That's why I don't want you to say anything about it. She's living in a cave not far from the river, and wouldn't leave it for the world. The only trouble is that she's lonely and wants a companion. Immediately I saw you I thought, "There's the very donkey for her. It couldn't be better".'

'Yes. Yes, of course,' Donkey said impatiently. 'Er—shall we leave right away?'

And so Fox and the lion's dinner went off together into the forest.

The lion had not long settled down when he heard voices outside the cave.

'She's in there,' someone was saying. 'You go in first and I'll follow.'

'No,' replied his companion. 'It wouldn't be right to go into a lady's house without a proper introduction.'

'Yes, it would. Go on.'

Lion edged towards the door. Outside he saw Fox talking to a donkey.

'That'll be my dinner,' he thought, and instantly he sprang through the opening of the cave. But the sudden light on his eyes made him misjudge the distance, and instead of landing on top of Donkey he soared right over him and disappeared into a thicket beyond. Donkey, alarmed by this sudden whirlwind, took fright, and before Fox, Lion or anyone else could stop him turned and fled. Fox stood eyeing Lion impatiently as he crept out of the thicket.

'I—I don't miss very often,' he said apologetically. 'I—I must be getting out of practice.'

'Well, wait until he comes into the cave next time,' said Fox sternly. He turned to go. 'He'll be back in about twenty minutes.'

'You surely don't expect him to return after this?'

'He'll be back,' replied Fox. And he ambled away.

Donkey was in the field where they had first met when Fox arrived.

'So there you are,' he said laughing. 'I've never seen

34

anything so funny in all my life. Whatever made you run off like that?'

'It—it was that fierce animal,' replied Donkey. 'It did give me a fright.'

'Fierce animal? What fierce animal?'

'Why, the one that jumped over my head.'

'Fierce animal? You don't mean—— Ha Ha Ha. That's a good one. That's a jolly joke, that is!'

'A joke?'

'Why, bless my soul, what would she think if she knew you'd called her a fierce animal? Why, she's the gentlest, most loving she-donkey in all the world.'

'But it jumped right over my——'

' "She," dear fellow, not "it". She did it accidentally. Too eager! That's been her fault all along. She heard us talking outside the cave and came to greet us. She didn't see that bit of loose turf in the entrance and tripped over it. And then what do you do? Instead of helping her to get up, you run away as if a—a lion were chasing you. I was terribly ashamed. I don't think she'll forgive you in a hurry.'

35

'Oh dear!' sighed Donkey.

'She's very sensitive indeed,' continued Fox. 'She can't stand bad manners in animals.'

'But I didn't know——'

'That doesn't make any difference. Poor girl! That's the sort of thing that always happens when you try to do someone a good turn. It almost makes you lose faith in animal nature.'

'Shouldn't I come along and say I'm sorry?' asked Donkey.

'It wouldn't do any good.'

'Oh please, I'm very very sorry. You see I didn't——'

'No! She's much too upset.' And with these words Fox turned back towards the forest. Donkey followed quickly.

'Please,' he begged, 'I didn't mean to——'

'It's no use.'

'But if only I'd have known I'd have——'

'I tell you it's too late. She says she never wants to see you again. And please stop following me.' But Donkey followed behind him still protesting.

At last they reached the lion's cave.

'This is the place, isn't it?' Donkey asked excitedly.

'Yes, it is,' replied Fox wearily. 'But I wouldn't go in if I were you.'

'I'm going in whether you like it or not,' said Donkey defiantly. And stopping only to flick the hair back from his forehead and run his tongue round his front teeth, he walked into the lion's den.

'That fox was a proper monkey,' said the Crow-King, laughing for the first time that morning.

'He was indeed,' replied White Wings.

'Mind you, it isn't always the trickster who comes off best,'

36

continued the King. 'Haven't you heard the story of the two brothers?'

THE TWO BROTHERS

There were once two brothers named Kon and Mon who lived in a small village in a Southern Province of India. The brothers were very poor indeed, their only possessions being a mattress, a cow and an apple tree, which they shared between them. But Kon, the elder brother, wasn't satisfied with this arrangement.

'Mon,' he said early one morning, prodding his brother who slept beside him on the mattress. 'Have a good night's sleep?'

'Eh—who—what—what's that you said?' asked Mon sleepily.

'I said, did you have a good night's sleep?'

'No, not very good. You had most of the blankets.' And he turned over to go to sleep again.

'I've been thinking,' continued his brother.

'Wh—what about?'

'I've been thinking that it would be a good idea if we had the mattress one at a time, instead of both together.'

'That's a good idea,' yawned his brother. 'But how do we do that?'

'Well, you can have it first from sunrise to sunset, and I'll have it from sunset to sunrise.'

'Th—that sounds like a good idea,' replied Mon, eager to get back to sleep.

That evening at sunset Kon settled himself comfortably in the centre of the mattress and prepared to go to sleep.

'What about me?' asked his brother.

'What do you mean, what about you?'

37

'Where do I sleep?'

'That's your concern. We agreed to let me have the mattress at sunset, and here I am. You'll have to sleep in the barn. You can have the mattress in the morning,' he added laughing.

'Mon,' said his brother next morning as they walked towards the shed in which their cow was tethered.

'What?'

'I've been thinking about the cow.'

'Have you?'

'Yes, I was wondering if it wouldn't be better for us to have half the cow each to look after.'

'How could we do that?'

'Well, you have the top half, and I'll have the bottom. Then we'd only have half the amount of work to do on it, and be finished twice as quickly.'

Mon was happy with this arrangement, particularly as he was extremely tired after his uncomfortable night in the barn. He led the cow into the shed, fed and tethered it and stood by while his brother got on with the milking at his end of the cow. At breakfast, however, he noticed that all the milk was on his brother's side of the table.

'May I have the milk, please?' he asked.

'Of course not,' came the reply. 'I look after the bottom half of the cow and all the milk belongs to me. I don't see why I should give away my property.'

Mon rose from the table at this. Although the younger of the two he was bigger than his brother and able to give a good account of himself.

'I'll tell you what I'll do,' said Kon hastily. 'We'll each have a share of the apple tree. You can have the bottom half, so you won't have to do any climbing. Now that's fair, isn't

38

it?' This sounded better to Mon and he sat down again.

That afternoon, Mon cleared the dead leaves from the foot of the tree and gave it some water, while his brother climbed the tree and picked the fruit.

'Throw me down an apple,' Mon called to his brother.

'Certainly not,' came the reply. 'The top half of the tree belongs to me and I don't see why I should give away my property.' And he stayed up the tree out of harm's way while his brother got on with his work below.

When they returned home that afternoon, the younger brother took the mattress out into the yard and before anyone could stop him soaked it thoroughly with water and began to lather it with a large bar of soap.

'What are you doing, you fool?' shrieked Kon.

'I'm just giving it a wash,' came the reply. 'It's getting very dirty.'

'But what about me? It'll be soaking wet when I go to bed tonight,' protested Kon.

'It's my property until sunset,' replied Mon pleasantly, 'and I can do anything I like with my property, can't I?'

'I've changed my mind about that arrangement,' cried Kon. 'I think it'd be better if we shared it as before.'

In the morning Kon went to the cowshed to milk the cow. Hardly was he seated on the three-legged stool when his brother came in with a large stick and began to beat the cow on the head with it.

'Stop it! Stop it, you idiot. Have you gone mad?' shouted his brother as the cow kicked over the pail and lashed him with her tail.

'What are you doing that for?'

'Why shouldn't I beat the cow? I own the top half, and as you yourself said I can do what I like with my own property.'

'I've changed my mind about that too,' stammered Kon. 'We'd better go back to our old arrangement.'

Kon was very bad-tempered over the business of the mattress and the cow.

'The apples are still mine,' he grumbled as he started to pluck them from the branches.

But no sooner had he begun to work than he heard a crash and felt the tree shake violently beneath him.

'What the—what's that?'

Looking down he saw his brother with an axe. 'What on earth are you up to now?' he yelled.

'I'm just chopping down the tree,' came the reply.

'But you can't do that.'

'I don't see why not. I'm not touching your part of the tree, am I? And I can do what I like with——'

'All right,' sighed his brother climbing down the tree.

40

'Put away your axe. I'll let you have your share of the apples.'

'Promise?' said Mon.

'I promise.'

And he kept his promise, although Mon kept a careful eye on him just the same from that time onwards.

'I wish,' said the Crow-King when he had finished the story, 'that everything ended as happily in life as it does in stories.'

'Sometimes it does, Your Majesty,' replied White Wings.

'Not with us. If things don't improve very quickly,' said the King, 'we'll have to leave our homes.'

'Surely not, Your Majesty.'

'What's to prevent the owls returning this very night and murdering us all in our nests?'

'I think I can, Your Majesty.'

'You?'

'Yes, I think I can.'

'You may ask me for anything you want,' began the King. 'You can have as many men and——'

'No, Your Majesty, this can only be done by one man.'

And he told the King his plan for ridding the crows of the terrible fear in which they lived.

2

The Plot

It was evening, and on the branches of a withering tree at the foot of the mountains sat the Owl-King surrounded by his advisers and followers.

'A few more raids like the one last night, Your Majesty,' the Owl General was saying, 'and our enemies will be forced to leave their city and take to the countryside.'

'That's exactly what I wish them to do,' said the King smiling. 'Then we can kill them one by one. Within a month there'll be no more crows left in the country.'

'Kill them all! Kill them all!' screeched Red-eye, a villainous old tawny owl with bloodshot eyes.

'We will, Uncle,' replied the King.

'Good! Good! I hate all crows, I hate 'em. If it wasn't for that saucy fellow my brother would have been King of All the Birds. Kill the lot! Kill them, I say.'

'Don't worry, Uncle, soon we'll be avenged for our wrongs. Soon there won't be a——' He stopped suddenly as a dark shape zigzagged uncertainly across the sky and dropped to the ground not far away. 'Hello! What's that?'

'A crow, Your Majesty,' said an attendant.

'Seize him!'

The guards hurried to the spot and dragged the exhausted crow before the King.

'Water! Water!' croaked the bird, a large fellow, all black except for two white patches half-way along each wing.

'Water? Fire rather!' screamed Red-Eye. 'Kill him! Kill all Crows.'

The King made a sign for the guards to take him away. But just at that moment one of the King's Counsellors came forward.

'Your Majesty,' he said, 'I recognize this crow. He is called White Wings and is chief adviser to his King. Perhaps he has come with an offer of surrender.'

The King turned to the prisoner.

'Are you indeed this White Wings?' he asked. 'Answer quickly, you are about to die.'

'Give me water,' pleaded White Wings. 'I've been on the wing all day and shall die if you don't give me something to drink.'

'Bring some water,' ordered the King.

Everyone gathered round as White Wings slowly drank the water. Then, he preened himself, straightening his crumpled feathers until he looked as smart and wise as any of the counsellors beside the King.

'Well?' asked the King impatiently. 'Have you come with terms of surrender?'

'No, alas, Your Majesty, though I've often advised my King to do that.'

'Then why are you here?' asked the King sharply.

'To offer my services to Your Majesty. I have been banished for advising my King to surrender. He called me the friend of the owls and has deprived me of my offices and taken away all my possessions. And so I have decided to offer you my services. Will you accept them, your Majesty?'

The King hesitated.

'Kill him! Kill him!' repeated Red-Eye who had been listening intently to the conversation. 'You can't trust a crow.'

'Spare him, Your Majesty.' The courtier who had first recognized White Wings approached the King. 'He may be of great service to you. He knows the inner councils of the crows and can advise us on all their movements.'

'He is a brave soldier,' added the Owl Commander generously. 'He has never been known to flee from battle, and has the courage of an owl.'

'Thank you for your kind words,' said White Wings. He turned to the King. 'If Your Majesty will spare my life, not only am I willing to serve you, but I shall become an owl subject and never again regard myself as a crow.'

'Nonsense!' cried Red-Eye. 'An owl's an owl and a crow's a crow. And that's all there is to it. No one can help being what he is. Have you never heard the story of the "Lion-Wolf"?'

'A Lion-Wolf?' repeated the King. 'He must have been a strange animal. What was it all about?'

THE LION-WOLF

A lion and his wife out hunting one day came across a wolf cub who had wandered off and lost himself. Unaware of the dangers which kept the older and wiser members of his family safely hidden in their homes at certain times of the day, this cub sniffed his way happily through the undergrowth, and on seeing the lion ran joyfully towards him and began playing with him as he played with his own father. He

44

tugged his great tail and sank his little teeth into a fleshy part of his leg.

'What shall we do about him?' asked the lioness.

'Nothing,' replied her husband. 'What do you expect us to do with him?'

'But we can't leave him here. He won't survive the day.' She paused as she watched him pulling the lion's tail. 'Let's take him home with us,' she said suddenly. 'He'll make an excellent playmate for our children.'

'He wouldn't,' replied her husband. 'And there'll be trouble if we try to bring him up as a lion.'

But his wife pleaded and pleaded, until at last he agreed to allow the cub to come home with them for fear that a hawk or serpent might seize him when they had gone.

Many years passed. The wolf, who had been treated exactly like the other members of the family, and not knowing that he was any different from his two brothers, looked upon himself as a lion. What he lacked in strength he made up in cunning and lived very happily as one of the family.

One day he was out hunting with his brothers when they saw a wild elephant in a forest clearing, his trunk stretching high into the branches as he picked mango fruit.

'Let's hunt him,' said the eldest brother. And straightway the three excited animals began stalking their prey. But the nearer they got to the elephant the larger he became in their eyes. The Lion-Wolf was the first to see their danger.

'We can't attack that monster,' he cried. 'It'll trample us to death.'

'Nonsense!' replied his brother. 'We lions can attack anything.'

'Of course, if you're afraid,' sneered the younger brother, 'you can always run home to mother.'

45

'I'm not afraid,' snorted the Lion-Wolf. 'But I'm not a fool either. If you want to get yourself killed, go ahead. I'm going home.'

The brothers laughed and turned once more towards their prey. But during the time they had been talking the elephant must have decided that he'd eaten enough, for he was no longer beside the mango tree and was nowhere to be seen in the thick undergrowth of the forest.

The three animals walked home in silence, the lions angry at having lost their prey, and the Lion-Wolf at having been called a coward.

'What's the matter?' asked their mother not long after they returned. 'You haven't spoken to me or to each other since you came in.'

'Ask him,' said the older brother pointing angrily at the Lion-Wolf.

'Why ask me?'

'Because it was your fault!'

'Why, what happened?' asked their mother.

'They wanted to hunt a bull-elephant, and I stopped them,' replied the Lion-Wolf.

'He was afraid!'

'That's not true. I wasn't any more afraid than you were. I only pointed out that it was foolish to attack a fully grown elephant. That's just common sense.'

'It isn't. A lion can attack anything!'

'Not a bull-elephant.'

46

'Yes, it can!'

'A lion like father can perhaps,' argued the Lion-Wolf, 'but we're not big enough.'

'Yes, we are!'

'We aren't. It's just foolish to——'

'Stop this arguing,' interrupted their mother. 'In my opinion you're both right. A lion like father can attack a fully grown elephant. But you boys aren't quite big enough. But we'll have no more quarrelling.'

'I still think he's afraid,' said the elder brother defiantly.

'I wasn't.'

'Yes, you were.'

'I'll prove it. I'll fight you.'

'Stop it immediately!' cried their mother, suddenly afraid. 'I won't have you quarrelling like this. I'm ashamed of you.' Shamed by these words the lions and their wolf brother were silent.

That evening the Lion-Wolf made his way to a cave not far away rather than spend the evening with his brothers. As he lay there turning over in his mind the events of the day, he heard footsteps. Looking cautiously out to see who it was, he saw his mother waiting for his father to return.

'The children have been quarrelling,' he heard her say as soon as the lion appeared.

'Why, what's wrong?'

And she told him everything that had happened, the quarrel after the hunt and the Lion-Wolf's challenge to his brother. 'You were right after all,' she said. 'It was wrong to try to turn a wolf into a lion.'

The Lion-Wolf lay silently in the mouth of the cave listening eagerly to every word.

'I'm afraid so,' replied the lion.

'But what shall we do?'

'We'll have to send him away. It'll be for his own good. If he fights with his brother he'll be killed. I'll have a talk with him in the morning.'

The following day the father set out to look for his strange son. He searched the usual clearings in the forest where his sons played and also the caves where they sheltered from the midday sun. But he was nowhere to be found. His brothers had not seen him, nor had anyone else. For all had gone to bed at sunset and slept soundly until dawn. But if anyone had remained awake during the night they would have seen a young, almost fully grown wolf steal out of a cave after midnight and make his silent, careful way to another part of the forest. It was a part from which on every moonlight night could be heard a call, a loud sharp call which was made with the head uplifted and the eyes raised towards the moon. It was that part of the forest inhabited solely by wolves, and where few other animals ever chose to live.

The owls listened thoughtfully to the old man's story. And to many it seemed as if it contained the reason why White Wings should not be admitted to the fellowship of the owls.

'Of course,' said White Wings quickly seeing that things were going against him, 'I have no wish to live exactly like an owl. I wouldn't like the food you eat, nor could I hunt with you or see in the dark. But I can help you in many other ways. Besides, I have come to you for shelter and throw myself on your mercy. Have you not heard the story of the hunter who was shown mercy by the dove?'

'No,' replied the King. 'I have not heard that story. What was it about?'

48

Once there was a hunter who was hated for his cruelty not only by the animals and the birds, but even by his fellow men. Each day many cried for mercy and flapped hopeless wings in the meshes of his nets. All who saw him trudging through the forest with his traps whispered that Death was coming and remained in their nests and sang no songs.

One evening this fearsome hunter was returning home from the forest with full hunting bags when he was overtaken by a storm. The sky blackened and before he reached shelter, rain flooded into the forest turning the trees into waterfalls and tracks into swamps of mud. He flung himself and his bags under a tree. 'What luck!' he grunted. 'It looks as if I'll be here for the night.' He shook his head fiercely as water splashed on him from the branches overhead. Then he yawned. For he had been out since early morning. And despite the mud all around him, despite the shock of lightning and the explosions of thunder, he fell asleep.

'Where are you? Where are you?'

He had not been asleep very long when he heard a voice calling. 'Eh—wh—what?' he sat up quickly, his hand reaching for his bow.

'Huh! Must have been dreaming!' He lay down again.

'Where are you? Where are you?'

Looking in the direction of the sound he saw in a hole in the tree above his head a dove, small, all-white. Seizing his bow he fitted an arrow.

'Where are you? Where are you?' called the bird.

'Here! Here I am!' came a whispered answer.

The hunter lowered his bow astonished. For the second

49

voice came from the bag of dead birds not far away on the ground.

'What has happened?' called the dove again. 'I've been waiting since dawn. It's been so long.'

To this there was no reply. The dove, anxious, called again. 'Why don't you answer?'

'I—I'm here in this hunting bag on the ground.'

'Fly away quickly! Escape while you can,' she cried alarmed.

'I can't. My wings are pinioned.'

'Break the strands.'

'I can't, they're too strong.'

'Wriggle loose. Tear the bag. Force yourself through the top.'

'I've tried many, many times.'

At this she wept. 'Is there no way? No hope? Is there no mercy in this hunter?'

'None, none! He is a stone, a man unmoved even by death. There is no shred of mercy in him.'

'Wretch!' screamed the dove. 'If only I had the talons of a hawk! I'd tear him to pieces, gouge his eyes, I'd——' Fury choked the words in her throat. 'I know what I'll do,' she cried suddenly. 'I'll lead tigers and panthers to this place and leave them to——'

'Wife,' her husband's voice interrupted. 'Listen to me. I am dying. Will you grant me a last wish?'

'Dearest one, best of husbands, of course. What is the wish?'

'I want you to wake the hunter.'

'Wake him?'

'The tree is in a hollow which floods when it rains. If he stays there he'll drown.'

'Good! That'll save me the trouble of warning the——'

'Listen!' called her husband. 'I want you to save his life.'

'Save his life? I'd rather see him tormented by eagles, clawed by a tiger. I'd rather——'

'You promised to grant my wish,' cried her husband. 'There is greater unhappiness in his world than our own. For us there are always berries, fruit and sweet water. We have high trees in which to make safe homes and nurse our children. But this unhappy man lives in a hut. His wife and children hunger and are in rags and bring him no happiness. Do not add to the misery of the world. Show him mercy, even though he has shown us none.'

Silence followed these words. The winds were silent, the leaves and the whirling branches of the trees were stilled.

The hunter who had listened to all this opened his eyes and shook himself.

'I don't need a bird to wake me. I'll save myself.' And he tried to rise. 'Hello! What's holding me?'

51

His legs were rigid like sticks; there was no strength in his wrists, nor power in his muscles.

'What's wrong? What's holding me? Let me up! Help! Help! Let me up! The water's rising. I'll be drowned.'

Water seeped out of the mud holes, oozed silently from pool to pool. Small puddles joined others, the ground between them filling and rising higher and higher around his stricken body.

'Help! Help!' he shrieked, 'I'll drown.'

Looking up he saw a dove on the branches of a tree.

'Help! Come quickly! Save me!'

The dove made no move.

'Save me! Save me!'

The water rose higher and higher. He could feel it under his head, his back, his legs. 'I'll kill you for this,' he shrieked to the bird. 'There'll be nothing left alive in the forest when I've finished. I'll kill every bird, every animal, every creature, I'll——'

The water rose higher.

'I'll tear down your nests, crush every fledgling, I'll——' He succumbed to terror. 'Help me! Save my life. Don't kill me.' Then he glimpsed death. He was instantly silent. Turning his face towards the bird he murmured, 'No, do not save me. I have never shown mercy. I deserve to die.'

At that moment the bird flew silently from the branch and touched his forehead with her wing.

A falling leaf woke the hunter.

'What the—how—where——?' He sat up. 'What's happened to the water? Why didn't it——?'

But there was no water to be seen. It was a bright, clear morning. The leaves were rain-fresh, birds sang on gleaming branches.

'I must have been dreaming. What a strange night. I don't think I ever want to——' He left the sentence unfinished.

Picking himself up he looked unsteadily round him. Then he brushed some mud and dead leaves from his coat. And leaving the game bags and nets where they lay, made his way home never again to return to the forest.

'I shall be like that dove,' said the King when White Wings ended his story. 'From henceforward you may join my court and live with us in our city.'

'I am very grateful indeed, Your Majesty.' White Wings bowed. 'I wish that I were really one of your people and not the miserable outcast that I am.'

'People are always wishing for what is beyond their reach,' replied the King. 'Have you heard the tale of the Maiden and the Ratcatcher?'

THE MAIDEN AND THE RATCATCHER

There once lived in India a maiden who was so beautiful that she seemed more than human. Now this maiden loved Tom the village Ratcatcher who lived next door, and wanted to marry him. But her mother who was very thin, very talkative and very, very foolish, decided that she should marry, not an ordinary man, but the greatest being in the world. But who was the greatest being in the world? She thought about this for weeks and weeks, asked the advice of wise men, studied the oldest books she could find, listened attentively to all the speeches of all the politicians. But even after this she was no wiser than when she had begun. Then one day she had an idea.

'Of course. Why didn't I think of it before!'

'Think of what?' asked her husband.

'Why, the sun!'

'What are you talking about?'

'The sun must be the greatest being in the world. He's much more important than the King. If the King doesn't get up in the morning, nobody's any the worse for it. But if the sun decided not to rise one morning the world would come to an end.'

'True,' agreed her husband, smiling to himself. 'He'd make an excellent "sun"-in-law.'

'Can't you ever be serious?' cried his wife. 'Anyway, I've set my mind on it, and we're going to visit the sun this very evening and offer him the hand of our daughter in marriage.'

Now to speak to the sun you have to go to the farthest end of the earth and wait for him at sunset. And every evening many people come to ask him questions and get him to make all sorts of promises. Farmers want him to shine for as many hours as possible, wise men want to know all about the universe, and priests are always asking him to pass on messages to their gods. And it was very late indeed before the couple were able to speak to him.

'Y-your Majesty,' stammered the husband nervously, 'my wife and I wish to offer you the hand of our daughter in marriage. She is the most beautiful maiden that ever was, and a fit wife for the greatest being in the world.'

'The greatest being in the world, eh?' The sun laughed

54

when he heard this. 'Thank you for the compliment. But I'm sorry to say you've made a mistake. I'm not the greatest being in the world. If only I were!' he sighed. 'I'd soon make some changes. You just don't know what I have to put up with. Why, there are days when I dread having to get up in the morning.'

The husband was astonished at these words. 'But why?' he asked.

'Why? Because of the clouds, of course. They make my life unbearable. You know, sometimes they won't even allow me to shine properly. They gather so thickly round me that I just can't see where I'm going. No! I'm certainly not the greatest being in the world. There'd be some changes if I were.'

When he had said this he disappeared over the edge of the world, leaving the father and mother to make their disappointed way home in the dark.

But the very first thing next morning the mother got up and put on her best clothes and perfumes.

'Where are you off to?' her husband asked sleepily.

'We,' replied his wife, 'are going to speak to the clouds.'

'The clouds? Whatever for?'

'I've been thinking about what the sun told us. If the clouds can really stop him shining, then they must be the greatest beings in the world.' And before he could even think of a reply she hustled him out of bed to come with her to meet the clouds.

Now this meeting proved easier than their meeting with the sun. For not very far away from their house was a small hill, the top of which seemed to be a favourite gathering-place for the clouds. They hung lazily overhead, taking very little notice of the couple.

'Good morning,' said the father, peering upwards toward the thickest part of the cloud gathering. 'My wife and I have decided to offer you the hand of our daughter in marriage. She is very beautiful and worthy of the greatest beings in the world.'

The clouds, which a few moments before were hanging idly over their heads suddenly sprang to life, making swishing noises like steam coming out of a kettle. The couple were quite frightened.

'The greatest beings in the world?' they hissed. 'Phew! That's very funny indeed.' They whirled about hissing and chortling. 'If you only knew how we're bullied, you wouldn't say such a thing.'

'Bullied?' asked the father. 'Who bullies you?'

'The wind! It has only to puff ever so slightly to send us scrambling from one part of the world to the other. And there's nothing we can do to stop it. If you only knew how we get ordered about! One moment we're basking in the sun, and the next we're shivering with cold on the other side of the world. Every command must be obeyed without question. We never know where we'll be from one day to the next. We certainly aren't the most powerful beings in the world. We'd give the wind something to think about if we were.' And delighted with this idea, they hissed and swirled about so fiercely that the couple ran down the hill alarmed.

'Oh dear!' complained the mother. 'It doesn't look as if we're ever going to find a husband for our daughter.'

They were sitting outside their house enjoying the sunshine and discussing their problems.

'Of course we shall,' replied her husband. 'There's always Tom the Ratcatcher. He wants to marry——'

'We haven't finished yet,' interrupted his wife. 'If the sun says the clouds are the most important beings in the world, and the clouds say that the wind is, our next move is to make an offer to the wind.'

'Psst!' A little breeze which happened to be passing at that moment overheard their words and thought he ought to give them some advice. 'Psst!'

But they went on with their discussion, not realizing they had a visitor.

'Psst! Psst!'

They couldn't see the breeze, but they could hear it, for it was puffing right into their ears.

'Psst! I couldn't help overhearing what you were saying about the wind,' whispered the breeze. 'He likes to believe he's the most important being in the world, but he isn't really.'

'Isn't he?' asked the father.

'No! He gets his own way with the clouds because they haven't a leg to stand on. But just you ask the wind to blow over a mountain. Then you'll see just how strong he is.'

Having given them this little piece of useful information the breeze whistled on his way before either the man or his wife could thank him.

'A mountain,' said the mother thoughtfully as soon as their visitor had gone. 'We could do much worse than marry our daughter to a mountain, very much worse.

And he'd make her a fine strong husband too.'

'And he isn't likely to run away and leave her either,' added the father.

And so they chose the highest mountain they could find, for only the largest one was good enough for their daughter.

'What was that you said?' asked the Mountain sleepily when they had made him the same offer they had made to the sun and the clouds and had almost made to the wind.

'We said, would you like to marry our daughter?'

'Carry off your daughter?' yawned the Mountain. 'No, I haven't carried off your daughter. I haven't seen anyone for the last two years. Maybe she's wandered off into some other mountain. Little girls are always getting lost.'

'We haven't lost our daughter. We asked if you would like to——' They stopped as a large cavern near the top of the Mountain opened wide and gave a mighty yawn that echoed in the valleys for some minutes.

'What's the matter?' asked the father. 'You look as if you haven't had any sleep recently.'

'Any sleep?' repeated the Mountain. 'That's a good one. I haven't been able to sleep for two hundred years.'

'Why?'

'Rats!' replied the Mountain.

'I beg your pardon?'

'Rats! They're a pest. They scurry in and out of my slopes, gnawing and nibbling my sides. I'm never left in peace. Sometimes I wish the ground would open and swallow me up. Then at least I'd be able to have a rest.'

The couple looked at each other.

'If the rats can upset him so much,' whispered the mother, 'they must be more powerful than even he is.'

'But we can't marry our daughter to a rat,' protested her

husband. 'What would the neighbours think!' He paused for a moment. 'But there is someone more powerful even than the rats.'

'Who?'

'Why, Tom next door. He's the best Ratcatcher there is. And he loves our daughter,' he added slyly.

'So he does. And to think I wouldn't let him marry our daughter because he was only a Ratcatcher. Silly of me, wasn't it?'

'Yes, very silly,' agreed her husband with a grin.

It had grown dark while the Owl-King was telling his story. White Wings, a bird of the day, was beginning to feel drowsy and long for his nest in the banyan tree. Then came a call.

'To the Secret City!' And one by one the owls swooped from the branches of the mountain trees towards the mysterious owl city which the Crow-King and White Wings were so eager to discover.

White Wings followed the owls for what seemed to him many, many hours. So dark was it that he had to listen for the flapping of their wings to guide him. He was becoming more and more drowsy and wanted only to perch somewhere in one of the trees and sleep until daybreak. Suddenly he heard a long call. The owls circled and dropped one after the other into a huge tree. It was like any other large tree, its tall bark free of branches below a great head of leaves. White Wings flew in cautiously, feeling the way with his wing tips. Then he stopped amazed. For inside the thick circles of leaves he saw perched on leafless branches row upon row of owl houses, tall round towers with windows, doors and chimneys. The towers became taller and taller as they approached the middle of the tree. And there in the very centre stood the largest of them all, the Palace of the King perched securely on the fork where the strongest branches met.

'So this is the famous City of the Owls,' thought White Wings, excited to be the first crow ever to set claw in this forbidden sanctuary. 'At least now I know exactly what I'm up against. It always helps,' he yawned. And as he lay in a hastily constructed nest near the outer walls of the city, he thought of a story which seemed to fit his present situation well.

THE CAVE THAT TALKED

Once there was a goat, a well-fed, saucy fellow with a pointed beard and sharp eyes. Being a bachelor he lived alone in a cave in the hills, but he liked nothing better than to spend the evening eating and drinking in good company, and it was often not until the early hours of the morning that he would return to his cave in the hills.

Now it happened that one night a lion discovered the entrance to his cave, and seeing a pile of grass and vegetable roots stored carefully in one of the corners, decided to wait for the owner to return. And he settled himself as comfortably as he could in the low narrow tunnel near the entrance.

It was a little after midnight when the gay bachelor returned. He had had a jolly evening talking, laughing and drinking mango wine with some people he had met by the river and was in a blissful, tipsy mood. But he wasn't too tipsy to realize that something was not quite right. Whether it was that the bushes had been disturbed, or that things

60

were too quiet, he didn't know. But something was wrong.

'Cave!' he called suddenly. 'Are you asleep?'

The lion inside lifted his head. 'Did the fool really expect the cave to answer?'

'Cave!' continued Goat, 'I've had an excellent evening. Would you like to hear about it?'

There was silence.

'You're not very talkative this evening, are you? Ah well, I expect you're tired. It's been a very warm day. Do you remember that goat with the twisted horn who spent the night here three weeks ago? Well, I met him down by the river with some friends. They invited me to spend the evening with them. Charming people!'

He paused as if waiting for the cave to make some comment, but hearing nothing continued with his story.

'One of them was a most aristocratic Red Deer, wonderful manners—used to belong to the Emperor's herd. Turtle was there too. You remember Turtle, small chap, thick-skinned, very bald. There's not a lot he doesn't know about what goes on in the river. You'd be surprised what those fishy fellows get up to. I was. He told an excellent story about what happened at a crab supper last week. Would you like to hear it?'

Silence.

'Well, would you?'

Still no reply.

'Look here,' said Goat, annoyed, 'either you're interested or you're not. I'm not going to waste my time talking to a dumb cave. If you haven't the good manners to reply, I'm—' he paused. 'I say, nothing's wrong, is it?'

The lion listened to all this with growing curiosity.

'Why is he talking to the cave?' he asked himself. 'Anyone

with the smallest brain knows that a cave can't talk. Why then is this goat trying to make conversation with it? And what does he mean by asking the cave to let him know if anything was wrong?'

'Well, is there?' asked Goat.

Silence.

'I suppose you remember our agreement, don't you?'

'What agreement?' wondered the lion.

'You agreed to warn me if there was any danger. It was part of our contract when I took up lodgings with you. You agreed to call out every night when I returned to let me know if everything was all right. And now you're breaking the contract. I've a good mind to take you to court. How am I to know that my life isn't in danger, eh? I don't feel like coming in at all tonight.'

Lion became worried. He had waited a long time for his supper. 'Maybe this cave does speak?' he thought. But that was absurd. Any reasoning animal knew that. Still, here was this goat, a well-educated, intelligent creature talking to it as if to anyone else.

'All right!' called Goat finally, 'don't answer. But I'm not coming in. I'll go and spend the night with my friend the goat with the twisted horn, and warn everybody that you're a cunning, dishonourable fellow. You don't deserve to house respectable company. Good-bye!' And he turned to go.

The lion hastily made up his mind. 'Don't go,' he called. 'Everything's all right. I didn't reply because I—I was tired.'

He said this as quietly as he could and trying to disguise his voice. But quiet as it was, it was still a roar and unmistakably the voice of a lion.

'That's better,' called Goat. 'I'm pleased to hear that you had the good grace to keep your word. Now I won't be a minute. I just want to collect a few pieces of grass for breakfast, and I'll be in right away.'

And off he sped as quickly as he could to the safety of the home of his friend the goat with the twisted horn.

'Now I know exactly what I'm up against,' thought White Wings, as he settled down for the night. And at daybreak when the owls were asleep in their homes he flew to the banyan tree to consult with his master and tell him of his plans.

3

The Story Ends

White Wings carried out many errands for the King of the Owls. He had to keep the crows under observation during the day, and report to the King any important changes which were taking place, all of which he did most faithfully —except that he watched the crows from the balcony of his master's Palace, and gave the owls the kind of information that was no use to them whatsoever. Nevertheless he was rewarded handsomely for his services and was permitted to move his home from the gates of the city nearer to the centre where all the important people lived. At first his nest was of a modest size. But as he grew in favour, so the size of his nest grew. Bigger and bigger it grew, bigger and bigger, until it was an enormous mansion of twigs, grass and dried leaves in one of the most exclusive parts of the town.

'What's he building that huge nest for?' Red-Eye asked the King one night when the two were sitting talking on the Royal Branch.

'He's always lived in that kind of luxury, I suppose,' came the reply.

'He's up to something.'

'It's your suspicious mind,' answered the King. 'He's been a great deal of use to us in the last few weeks. He's told me of every move that's been made in and out of the banyan tree, the strength of their defences, what the King intends to do about our raids, how they are going to——'

'What's that you said?' interrupted Red-Eye suddenly.

'I said, or rather I was about to say, that they were going to evacuate the whole of the outer part of the——'

'No, before that.'

'He told me what the King intends to do about our raids.'

'How does he know that?'

'I expect he just kept his ears open.'

'He must have very long ears to hear what's going on in the Royal Palace.'

'What do you mean?'

'How can he know what the King has decided unless he spoke to him?'

'Maybe he did.'

'Do you imagine the King would reveal state secrets to a traitor?'

'I didn't think——'

'Of course you didn't.'

'Guards!' The King's loud call shook the leaves of the trees. 'Fetch the crow White Wings to me this instant.'

White Wings was standing outside his mansion when a furious beating of wings warned him that he was about to have visitors, and not very friendly visitors either.

'His Majesty wishes you to come to the Palace immediately,' snapped the Owl Commander of the Guard.

'Certainly,' smiled White Wings disarmingly. 'I expect he has another errand for me to perform.'

'I don't know about that. But you're to come immediately.'

'Of course. I'll just get my cape and I'll be out in a second.'

Once inside the house White Wings hurried towards a heap of faggots piled high in the centre of the floor. Quickly he seized a burning brand from the fire and threw it into the pile. Then he darted out through a door at the back.

'Hurry up,' called the Guard Commander.

There was no reply.

'Come out this instant, do you hear? His Majesty commands that you come to the Palace immed——'

The rest of the word never arrived. For at that very moment flames roared out of the vast nest. It was a beacon lighting the entire city.

'Fire! Fire!' shrieked the Guard Commander. 'Bring the fire engines.'

'They'll need more than fire engines to stop that,' thought White Wings as he flew out of the city.

He was right. The fire quickly caught the near-by branches, and one after the other they exploded into flame. Soon the whole tree, its tower houses, public buildings, the Royal Palace itself were blazing. The whole secret city of the owls died in the fire.

White Wings was given a hero's welcome when he returned. Crow orchestras played, and crow chicks sang songs and threw flowers and petals on his head as he flew by. It was a national holiday, a holiday which has been held ever since. And on that day crows tell their children the story of the hero White Wings and how he discovered, and all on his own destroyed, the secret city of the owls.

PART TWO
THE TWO FOXES

1

The Fear of The Lion King

It all started a long time ago when a merchant was making a journey with his wagon teams through the forests of Kamaka to a market town in the Northern Provinces of India. It had been a very wet season and the forest tracks were muddy and deeply rutted. Impatient to arrive early at the market the merchant urged his wagon teams faster than they could go, and the leading bullock, a king amongst his kind, stumbled suddenly into a ditch. Angry with the delay the merchant ordered his servants to drag the bullock out very quickly.

'It's no use, master,' said the foreman after several attempts had been made. 'We can't move him. We'll have to unyoke a team of bullocks from the other wagons to pull him out.'

'We haven't time for that,' replied the merchant impatiently. 'The important market buyers will be gone by the time we arrive. We'll just have to leave him where he is. Lead on.' And despite the pleas of the foreman not to abandon so fine an animal, he urged the procession forward, leaving the unfortunate bullock alone and in great pain in the ditch by the roadside.

Now it happened that the Lion King of the forest was passing not very far away when he heard the roars of the injured bullock. It was an unfamiliar and frightening sound, and the Lion King, who was really a shocking coward, was very much afraid. Not wishing to appear so, however, he suggested to his followers that they retire to his cave to discuss the matter. What was this strange monster? Would he be a rival to the Lord of the Jungle? These were the questions which troubled the Lion King most.

'Where are Damanaka and Karataka, my Ministers of State?' The Lion King turned to a servant. 'Tell them to come to me this instant.'

'But Your Majesty,' replied the attendant, 'they are no longer here. You banished them from your royal presence only last night.'

'Did I? Oh, I forgot. Er—what did I banish them for?'

'I—I don't know, Your Majesty.'

'Well, it doesn't matter. Send them to me immediately.'

'Yes, Your Majesty.' And the attendant went to the home of the banished ministers to command them to come into the royal presence.

'I wonder what he wants us for,' Damanaka said when the message arrived.

'His usual panic,' replied Karataka. He took a measured bite out of his breakfast banana and the two foxes went calmly on with their meal.

'The messenger says we're to go immediately,' Damanaka said a few minutes later. 'It must be important.'

'It never is,' replied his friend. 'It's probably just another of his strange ideas. Remember the time he woke us at four o'clock in the morning to show us the coconut which he thought was a piece of heaven that had fallen on his head? He's always panicking about something or other. Anyway, we can't go this time. We've been banished.'

70

'So we have. I forgot. Er—what shall we do?'

'Nothing in a hurry,' replied Karataka, taking another bite from the banana. 'We know what sort of a person our King is, and how oddly he behaves at times. It's not always wise to be too willing to help. You remember what happened to the hermit who was so full of good advice, don't you?'

'No, what happened?'

Karataka the Cunning, chief advisor to the Lion King, settled himself comfortably and began his story.

THE HERMIT AND THE SEA OF MAN

Once there lived in the town of Ujjain an Emperor named Darma-Dala. He was a just and wise ruler, and wishing to provide his people with water during the season of drought, he ordered the best engineers in the country to construct a huge water tank. It was the wonder of the age. The palace itself, the temples with their high pinnacles, even the great mountains to the north of the kingdom might well have been swallowed up if put in its waters. So wide was the expanse that it was impossible to see one shore from the other, except on the clearest of days. It was well named the Sea of Man.

For some weeks all went well, and everyone congratulated the engineers on the success of their task. One day, however, it was noticed that the level of the water was lower than on the day before. And on the next day it had dropped again. Day after day the water continued to drain away from the tank. The Emperor ordered the engineers to repair the leak, but so huge was the tank that it could not be found. Finally he offered a reward to any person in the kingdom who could prevent the Sea of Man from running dry.

Now there lived in the forest not very far away from Ujjain

an aged hermit. This hermit, far from becoming a wiser man
in the quiet shelter of the forest, grew daily more foolish. He
was in fact a silly busybody of a man who never failed to
give advice, whether it was asked for or not. And his advice
was always the same. If it rained too hard he said that the
gods were angry and advised people to make sacrifices to
them. If the sun shone too brightly and burnt the crops, he
again advised people to make sacrifices. If the crops didn't
grow, the animals were sick, if there was an accident, if
people suffered some misfortune, died, were born, or were
about to be married, he always had the same remedy. Make
sacrifices to the gods! And no sooner had news of the royal
proclamation reached him than, hoping for some gain, he set
off for the palace full of advice for the Emperor.

He was greeted courteously. The Emperor rose from his
throne to welcome the aged Holy Man, and kissed the hem of
his long robes.

'I have come to see you about the Sea of Man, Your
Majesty,' began the hermit.

'If you have any suggestions to make I shall be only too
pleased to——'

'The reason the tank is running dry,' continued the old
man, interrupting him, 'is that the gods are angry that you
have disobeyed their wishes.'

'Disobeyed their wishes?' repeated the Emperor. 'How
have I done that?'

'This way, Your Majesty. It is the gods who make the
weather, is it not?'

'It is.'

'The gods send the sun, the rain, the wind and the snow?'

'They do.'

'Now, you have built this tank in order to prevent people

suffering from the drought, have you not?'

'I have.'

'But the gods also send the drought. And by trying to avoid it, you have disobeyed their wishes.'

The Emperor stared amazed at the foolish old man.

'What do you think I ought to do about it then?' he asked patiently.

'The answer is simple. Since you have disobeyed the gods you must make a great sacrifice to show that you still respect them.'

'What shall I sacrifice to them?'

'A human life,' came the astonishing reply.

At this the Emperor could bear to listen no longer. 'Thank you for your advice, Holy Man,' he said politely. 'I shall think about what you have said and shall decide what to do when I have heard all my other advisers.'

And advice the Emperor certainly did have. Some suggested bringing up the water level by filling the tank with stones, others that the water should be frozen hard to prevent its running away, and others that every citizen should empty a bucket of water into the tank as he left his home in the morning. But the experiments failed. Stones were put in the tank to help fill it up, but they made the water dirty and unfit to drink. They had to give up trying to freeze the water because the sun thawed it out very quickly after sunrise. Citizens had to be stopped emptying their buckets into it every morning when it was discovered that some of them used it as an excuse to get rid of their household rubbish. The Emperor was desperate.

'What shall I do? What shall I do?' he asked himself. And then he remembered the advice of the hermit. 'I wonder if the old man was speaking the truth after all?' he thought. 'I wonder if——' he stopped as a sudden thought came to him. 'Send for the hermit immediately,' he ordered.

'I have been thinking,' said the Emperor when the hermit arrived, 'that we might try your suggestion of a sacrifice.'

'I thought Your Majesty would come to understand the wisdom of my words. It's not often that I make a mistake,' replied the silly old man, 'but people, alas, take very little notice of me. As I was saying only yesterday——'

'Yes! Yes!' said the Emperor. 'So I have decided to make a human sacrifice to the gods whom I have offended.'

Again the hermit was ever ready with advice. 'The person will have to be sacrificed at dawn when the gods are rising from their beds,' he advised.

'The best time,' agreed the Emperor.

'It must be a man.'

'Quite so.'

74

'A man furthermore, whose services are of no use to the state.'

'Of course.'

'A person who has neither parents nor relatives who might wish to avenge his death.'

'Naturally.'

'A man who will go willingly to his death for the love of his Emperor and the good of his country.'

'Exactly what I was thinking.'

'Er—has your Majesty anyone in mind?' asked the hermit, delighted that the Emperor had taken all his advice,and seeing himself already as a future Minister of State and power behind the throne.

'I have,' replied the Emperor.

'May I ask Your Majesty who it is?'

'You may.'

'Who is it, then?'

'You.'

'Me?'

'That was the last word the hermit spoke before he fainted,' said Karataka. 'In fact it was the last word he ever spoke at all in this world. Because on the following morning at sunrise, while the gods were still fresh from their night's sleep, he was thrown, after a very imposing ceremony attended by all the most important people in the kingdom, into the lake.'

'Did it do any good?' asked his friend who was listening thoughtfully to the story.

'As a matter of fact it did. You see there was a hole in the tank and the robes of the hermit wedged themselves tightly into it and prevented the water from running away.'

'The old busybody did some good then,' smiled Damanaka

when the story was finished, 'which was more than the talkative tortoise ever did.'

'The talkative tortoise? I don't think I've heard about that.'

'Well, I'll tell you if we have the time.'

'We have as much time as we want,' chuckled the other. 'The King can't do anything without us, and——'

'He can't do anything with us either,' added Karataka.

THE TORTOISE WHO TALKED TOO MUCH

There was once a Tortoise who talked too much. He was forever poking his nose into everyone's business, telling lengthy stories of his own adventures, and saying the first thing that came into his head. What a chatterer he was! He talked from the moment he poked his head out of his shell in the morning to the moment he put it back in again at night. And sometimes even then he could be heard mumbling to himself. Some said he was talking in his sleep, others, less kindly, that he just couldn't stop talking even when he was by himself.

'How are we going to stop him?' Cat, who had been very annoyed by the gossip he had been spreading about her, asked Porcupine one day.

'We'll have to talk to him about it,' replied Porcupine.

'It won't do any good. He's much too thick-skinned to take any notice.'

But Porcupine thought this would be the best thing to do, and the very next morning he went to pay Tortoise a visit.

Tortoise lay under a pile of dried leaves outside his house watching everyone as they passed and listening to any scraps of conversation he might be fortunate enough to overhear. He saw Porcupine coming in the distance and started talking to him as soon as he was near enough to hear.

'Hullo, Porcupine, old chap. Have you heard about He Goat and the pumpkin?' And before Porcupine could say anything at all he rambled on with the story.

'Well, it all happened like this. The other day He Goat saw a pumpkin which he mistook for a dangerous enemy. He charged it with his head, and what do you think happened? His horns became all——'

'Tortoise!' shrieked Porcupine as loudly as he could in order to make himself heard, 'that's just what I've come to talk to you about.'

'What? About He Goat?'

'No! About you.'

'But I didn't put my head through a pumpkin.'

'I know you didn't.'

'Then why did you say I did?'

'I didn't. I said I wanted to talk to you about yourself.'

'What about myself?'

'I wanted to ask you not to talk so much about other people.'

'Did He Goat ask you to do that?'

'No.'

'Are you sure he didn't?'

'Of course I'm sure.'

'Then why are you taking his side?'

'I'm not taking his side!'

'Yes, you'll be saying next he didn't put his head through the pumpkin.'

'I won't.'

'There you are, you admit it. He did put his head through the pumpkin,' cried Tortoise in triumph. 'It's just as I said. I heard She Goat telling Bat only yesterday that——'

But Porcupine was no longer listening. He crept slowly away holding his aching head in his paws. Cat had been right after all. Tortoise was much too thick-skinned to understand what was being said to him. Tortoise for his part hadn't noticed that Porcupine had gone.

'And that's the story as I heard it from She Goat's own lips. Don't tell her that I told you. She wouldn't want the farmer to know that it was He Goat who destroyed the pumpkin.' He turned to go into his house. 'Well, good-bye, Porcupine, old chap. It's been so nice having this little conversation with you. But I've got to be going now. Tiger will be along soon and I want to hear all that he has to say for himself.'

And with these words he left his invisible companion and returned to his pile of dried leaves to wait for Tiger and for the news he was going to bring.

That Summer there was a great drought in the country. The trees looked a stony brown, the ground as harsh and flakey as a dried coconut skin, and the pools and rivers where the animals went to drink had barely enough water for the sparrows to have their daily bathe.

'We'll have to go somewhere else for our water,' said a crane to his brother one morning as they were passing Tortoise's dwelling place.

'I know a pool in the mountains where there's always water,' replied his brother. 'We can fly there this afternoon.'

Tortoise who, of course, had been listening to their conversation, came out from beneath his pile of leaves.

'Will you take me with you?' he asked. 'I haven't had a good drink for a fortnight and my shell's getting as hard as flint.'

'How can we take you?' asked the older crane. 'You're much too heavy for me to carry you on my back.'

'It's easy,' replied Tortoise. 'Carry a strong stick between you in your beaks and I'll hold on to it with my teeth.'

78

The cranes looked at each other and smiled. Everyone knew his reputation as a great talker. How could he be expected to stay silent for the hour or more that the journey would take?

'If you travel that way you won't be able to talk,' said the older crane.

'Don't worry about that,' replied Tortoise, 'I know when to hold my tongue. No one could ever accuse me of being a chatterbox.' Once again the cranes looked at one another. And it was all they could do not to burst out laughing.

And so that afternoon the cranes carried Tortoise between them towards the mountains. They flew high over the country. The ground below was covered with a blue heat haze and it was impossible to distinguish the forests from the plains. On and on they flew over the growing foothills, until the highest range of all. After a while they came in sight of a large mountain lake. Their journey was almost ended. Tortoise was silent the whole time. He had, of course, been watching eagerly everything going on around him, prying into the nests of the eagles high up in the mountains, listening to the conversations of other birds as they flew by, and eaves-dropping on the chatterings of the skylarks. All this information he stored up as future gossip. He found it very hard not to talk to the cranes as they flew along. He wanted to tell them which way he thought they ought to go, remind them to be back before nightfall, and give them all kinds of advice that they knew very well for themselves. But he had to hold firmly on to the stick. They were flying over the lake in the mountains when Tortoise suddenly thought of something else. If the cranes drank too much water after having been so long without, it was certain to do them harm. He had better warn them not—— But the moment he opened

his mouth he lost his hold on the stick. Down he fell. Down, down. Then with an enormous splash he hit the water. The cranes dived quickly after him and were just able to pull him out before he sank.

Poor Tortoise was in a terrible state. Shivering after his icy bath, he lay on the bank scarcely able to breath through his chattering teeth. The cranes covered him as well as they could with their wings, and when he was strong enough to hold the stick flew back with him, stopping every now and again to allow him to rest.

'I need hardly tell you,' said Damanaka coming to the end of his story, 'that Tortoise didn't open his mouth more than he had to after that. Cat, He Goat, Tiger, Porcupine were very relieved, and so were all the other animals who didn't care to have their private affairs discussed with everyone else by the talkative Tortoise.'

'Er—what shall I tell His Majesty?' asked the messenger, who all this while had been standing listening to the Ministers' stories.

'Tell him that my friend and I are in consultation,' replied Karataka, 'and will come as soon as possible.'

'Perhaps, sir, if I may be so bold as to make a suggestion, one of you might like to come with me. The King will be angry if neither of you obeys his command.'

'My son,' replied Karataka seriously, 'I see that you have a great deal to learn about the ways of the world. When people are in trouble it is always safer to have an ally. Have you never heard the story of the pilgrim and the crab?'

'No sir, I haven't.'

'I'll tell it to you before we leave.'

THE PILGRIM AND THE CRAB

Once there lived in the town of Samapuri a man named Karla Sarma. He was a kindly man well known for his generous deeds. Not only did he befriend the poor but also the animals, birds and even the fish in the rivers. One day when he was on a pilgrimage he was approached by a crab which climbed up on to the banks of a river he was crossing and greeted him in a very polite manner.

'Good morning, Karla Sarma,' said the crab, bowing as he spoke.

'Good morning to you,' replied Karla smiling. 'But how did you know my na ne?'

'You are well known in these parts for your kindliness,'

replied the crab. 'Everyone speaks of you, the animals when they come to drink at the river, the birds on the trees beside its banks and the fish in the waters.'

'I am pleased that they all think so well of me,' said Karla. 'But what can I do for you?'

'There is something troubling me very much,' said the crab.

'What is it?'

'It is this river. Every day more and more people seem to be getting to know of it. It wouldn't be so bad if they only crossed and went on their way. But they linger here and throw their rubbish in the water. Women now come and

wash their clothes in it and children stir up the mud with their games. The water's getting so dirty that it's no longer possible to live here.'

'What would you like me to do?' asked Karla.

'I've heard that ten miles north of here is a quiet river known to only a few people. Would you take me with you in your haversack and leave me beside that river?' the crab asked.

'Of course,' replied Karla. 'I'm going that way and would like a little company.'

'Thank you,' said the crab gratefully. 'Your reputation for kindness is well deserved. I only hope that one day I shall be able to repay you in some way.'

Karla smiled at these words. 'How would you be able to help me?' he asked. 'We live in different worlds, you in the water and I on land.'

'That makes little difference to friends,' replied the crab. 'Have you never heard about the crow, the mouse, the deer and the turtle, and how they were able to help each other?'

'No,' replied Karla.

'Sit beside the river and rest for a while, and I'll tell you about the four friends,' said the crab.

THE FOUR FRIENDS

Once there were four friends, Mouse, Deer, Turtle and Crow. They lived happily together beside a lake in the forest. In the cool evenings they would stretch themselves comfortably upon the soft grass and the plantain leaves, and as their shadows lengthened over the water entertain one another with accounts of the day's happenings. Crow gave them all the news from the tree-tops, Deer from the forest, Mouse from the underground burrows and Turtle from beneath the waters of the lake.

One evening Crow, Mouse and Turtle sat beside the lake waiting for Deer.

'I wonder what's keeping him?' asked Turtle. 'He's never been as late as this before. I hope nothing's wrong.'

'I'm getting a bit worried too,' declared Mouse. 'Bat told me that there was a hunter somewhere in the forest.'

'In that case we'd better go and look for him,' said Crow. 'He may need our help.'

Away he flew. Mouse followed as quickly as he could, and Turtle stayed behind to look after their house.

It was Crow who first saw him. Deer was indeed in need

of help. He was trapped in a snare set by the hunter and had been struggling vainly since midday to free himself. And by the time Crow arrived he had given up hope.

'I'm so pleased to see you,' he sighed, 'but it's too late to do anything now.'

'Don't despair, Deer, old chap,' replied Crow comfortingly. 'Help is on the way. Mouse'll be here shortly and he'll have you out of the trap in no time.'

Mouse, being so small had been able to crawl under the bushes and through hedges, and very soon arrived. Quickly he started to gnaw through the ropes of the trap.

'Don't worry, don't worry,' he squeaked each time he stopped to breath, 'there aren't many ropes I can't get through.'

But it was a long job and took him nearly all the evening. So long was he in fact, that Turtle, who had grown tired of waiting at home, appeared on the scene.

'He's almost free,' Mouse told him, 'but you shouldn't have come. It's getting dark and the hunter's certain to come back to look at his traps. What would happen if——'

Crow suddenly gave a warning caw from the tree-top. 'He's coming! The hunter's coming.'

Deer found new strength from somewhere and managed to snap the final strands and scramble free just before the hunter arrived. Mouse scampered into a tiny hole. But it was not so easy for Turtle.

'What's this!' cried the hunter angrily, seeing his snare torn to pieces and his quarry gone.

'He must have gnawed his way out of—— Hullo!' he broke off, catching sight of Turtle trying vainly to push his way through a thicket beside the track. 'Here's a bit of luck.

84

I've never seen a turtle so far away from the water. It'll do for my supper instead of venison.' And seizing Turtle he tied him to his bow and started off home.

Deer and Mouse wept to see poor faithful Turtle being carried away in this fashion to the stewpot.

'It's all my fault,' said Deer. 'If I hadn't been so stupid as to fall into that trap, Turtle would be with us now.'

'If only he had waited,' said Mouse, 'this would never have happened.'

'It would be a better idea,' said the more practical Crow, 'to spend your time thinking of a way to free Turtle. While you've been blabbering I've had an idea. Now listen carefully and do everything I say, or Turtle will probably end his days in the hunter's stewpot.'

'I might have had nothing at all,' the hunter was saying to himself as he walked back home with Turtle strung to his bow. 'I haven't seen such a plump fellow as this for a long time. I'm very fond of turtle broth, and my wife likes nothing better. This fine fellow will keep us well supplied for——' He stopped suddenly. Lying on the ground some way in front of him he saw the body of a deer. Perched on the carcass was a crow pecking at it.

'This must be the animal that escaped from my trap,' cried the hunter. 'What luck! A deer and a turtle in the same day.'

He propped the bow with Turtle strapped to it beside a tree and ran forward to prevent the crow from doing too much damage to the carcass. But he was some time reaching the body, for the track in that part was overgrown, and the straggling roots got in the way. Finally, however, he reached the body. He was about to seize it and put it on his shoulders when an extraordinary thing happened. The dead animal

came suddenly to life and bounded away, while the crow
flew up high into the trees cawing loudly. The hunter was too
astonished to move. It was some minutes before he did
anything. Then he turned and made his way back to the
place where he had left his bow. He still had the turtle. That
was some comfort at least. That was better than—— But he
was in for yet a greater shock. For when he got back to the
tree the turtle had gone. The turtle, or so it seemed to him,
had gnawed its way through the ropes holding it prisoner.

'This place's haunted,' shrieked the hunter. 'I'm getting
home as quickly as I can.' And without waiting to pick up his
bow he ran as quickly as he could away from the forest in
which dead animals suddenly came to life and inland turtles

had teeth sharp enough to gnaw their way through thick ropes.

That evening on the banks of the lake a very happy Crow, Mouse, Deer and Turtle were preparing a feast to celebrate their safe homecoming. They collected the choicest fruits and vegetables, and ate, and drank their homemade wines until very late that night. And they celebrated the next night as well, and the night after that. And ever after they lived very happily, enjoying many dinners and cheerful conversations in their home beside the lake.

'So you see,' said the crab, 'we can all be of help in some way or other.'

Karla nodded in agreement, and putting the crab in his haversack started on his way.

It was midday when they reached a forest, and as the sun was directly overhead and extremely hot, Karla decided to rest in the shade and continue his journey later in the afternoon. He stretched himself out under a large banyan tree and was soon fast asleep.

Now there lived in the branches of that very tree a carrion crow who was in league with a serpent. Whenever a traveller passed that way the crow warned the serpent, and as soon as the serpent had killed him the two would share the spoils. And this is what happened. While the unfortunate Karla was alseep the serpent crawled out of its hiding place and bit him. The crow noticing the haversack put his head inside to find out what was in it. But as he groped around in the dark he suddenly gave a shriek. For a pair of steely pincers tightened round his neck. The cowardly serpent hurried away as soon as it heard the cry of alarm.

'Let me go! Let me go!' shrieked the crow.

But the crab held on tightly and would not let go.

'Let me go; you're strangling me.'

'Why should I let you go?' asked the crab bitterly. 'You have killed my friend. He was a good man who helped everyone who came to him. You deserve to die.' And he tightened his grip.

'Don't kill me,' pleaded the crow. 'Don't kill me and I'll save your friend. I'll suck the poison from the wound if you'll save my life.'

'Do it quickly,' ordered the crab. And so the crow sucked the poison from the wound.

It was a few moments before anything happened. Then Karla shuddered. He gave a little groan, then opened his eyes.

'I—I must have been asleep a long time,' he began. 'I don't remember ever——'

He stopped as he caught sight of the crow beside him with his friend the crab hanging on to its neck.

'What's happened?' he asked.

'This crow,' replied his friend, 'betrayed you to a serpent who tried to kill you while you were asleep. I made him draw the poison from the wound.'

'On condition that you spared my life,' added the crow.

'Spare your life!' retorted the crab. 'A life such as yours is not worth sparing.' And as he said this he tightened his grip on the scraggy, black neck of the crow.

'Spare me! Spare me!' implored the creature.

'How many travellers have you spared?' asked the crab. And with these words he gave the crow a final nip and put an end to its wicked life.

'Thank you for saving my life,' said Karla. 'Your repayment for my help came much sooner than I expected. But there is one thing worrying me,' he added in a serious voice.

'What is it?' asked the crab.

'Why, when you agreed to spare the life of the crow if he sucked the poison from my wound, did you put him to death?'

The crab was a few moments before replying. He looked first at the body of the crow, then into the eyes of Karla Sarma.

'The wicked are never to be trusted,' he replied thoughtfully. 'This creature would have gone running to the serpent for revenge as soon as our backs were turned. If I had spared his life we would have both lost our own. Have you not heard the story of the traveller and the tiger?'

'No,' replied Karla. 'Tell me about it while I am getting my strength back. I don't feel like going on for a little while.'

THE TRAVELLER AND THE TIGER

Once, a long time ago a traveller by the name of Astika was journeying through a small village on the banks of the river Jumna when he came upon an iron cage in which a tiger was imprisoned. Astika felt sorry to see so handsome a beast in a cage. But he reminded himself that tigers were the fiercest, most unreliable beasts in the forest, and concluding that it was better that the tiger should be shut up in the cage than free to roam in the forest through which he himself was about to travel, continued his journey. He had gone only a few steps, however, when he heard someone call.

'Excuse me,' said a polite voice.

He turned round quickly. No one was there, no one that is except the tiger in the cage.

'Excuse me,' repeated the voice. It was the tiger.

'Wh—what can I do for you?' Astika inquired.

'I'm sorry to cause you an inconvenience,' said the tiger. 'I see from your clothes that you are a pilgrim and I apologize for disturbing your pious thoughts at this moment.'

'Not at all,' replied Astika, astonished at the politeness of the tiger. 'But what can I do for you?'

'It's a small matter really,' replied the tiger. 'But I wonder if you would be good enough to release me. This is a very small cage, and I am rather a large tiger. We tigers like nothing better than to be free, to lie among the leaves and rub our backs against tree trunks. But as you see there are no leaves in this cage, and certainly no tree trunks. And I do need a drink badly. You will release me, won't you?'

While the tiger was speaking Astika stared unbelievingly at him. He'd never met one like this before—in fact, he'd made a point of meeting as few tigers as possible.

'I'm extremely sorry,' he replied. 'But what you ask is impossible.'

'Why is that?' asked the tiger, raising its eyebrows slightly.

'Because you and I are natural enemies. It is your duty to kill me, and mine to kill you.'

'My dear fellow,' said the tiger laughing heartily. 'I've never heard anything so funny for a long time. That's all a thing of the past. People don't really believe all that sort of thing nowadays.'

'Don't they?' asked Astika puzzled.

'Of course not. Now, you will let me out like a good chap, won't you?'

Shamed by the tiger's worldly remarks, and not wishing to be thought ignorant, Astika shot back the bolts of the cage. 'If you're sure it's all right—— Hey, what are you doing?'

The tiger, having leapt out of the cage suddenly reared up

in front of him and put its forelegs on his shoulders. Its face
was only a few inches away from his own, and its hot breath
was all there was for Astika himself to breathe.

'Wh—what are you going to do?' he asked alarmed.

'Eat you, of course,' replied the tiger casually.

'But you promised not to eat me.'

'No, I didn't. If you cast your mind back over our conversation, you'll discover that I gave no such guarantee.'

'But you said that tigers and men were no longer natural enemies. Y-you said that it was a thing of the past.'

'That's quite true,' replied the tiger, 'but it still goes on in out-of-the-way places—like this one. Progress always takes longer in these backward areas.'

'But you wouldn't do anything as uncivilized as that?' said Astika.

'Not normally,' agreed the tiger, 'but I'm extremely thirsty. And as doctors all agree that it isn't wise to drink on an empty stomach, I'm afraid I shall have to eat you first. I'm awfully sorry. But you wouldn't like me to get cramp, or stomach pains or anything like that, would you now?'

'Listen, my friend,' said Astika, seeing a chance to beat the tiger at his own game. 'A very short while ago you were imprisoned in that abominable cage from which I released you. I agreed to help you because you seemed a superior kind of fellow, and because I had no wish to see you made into a rug for somebody's wife. But for me you might have been dead by now. So consider. I saved you from being made into a rug, and what do you do? You spring at me, place your feet on my shoulders and threaten to eat me. Now is that gentlemanly? Is it fair?'

The tiger hesitated at these words. And seizing his opportunity, Astika continued. 'Let us go and ask four judges whether it is fair or not that you should eat me. If they agree with you, then I am willing to be your first meal out of captivity. If, however, they don't agree with you, you must release me.'

'All right,' said the tiger, without enthusiasm. And taking his paws from Astika's shoulders he padded sulkily beside him until they reached a clearing in the forest, where stood a large banyan tree, its trunk gnarled and rubbery like the face of a very old, wise man.

'Excuse me,' called Astika, tapping lightly on the bark of the tree to awaken it from its midday slumber. 'Excuse me! We would be very grateful if you could settle a dispute between us.'

'Eh—who—what's that you say?' called the old tree through a mouth somewhere in the branches above their heads.

Astika repeated his question, only more loudly because he thought that the old tree might be a little deaf.

'There's no need to shout,' called the voice angrily from above. 'I'm not deaf. Dispute you say? Dear me! You creatures are always having disputes. Why can't you be like us trees? We go on for hundreds of years without complaining. And heaven knows we've enough to complain about. But what is it? What's all the trouble about?'

'This tiger,' began Astika, 'was locked in a cage. As I passed by he explained that he was very uncomfortable and thirsty and assured me that he would do me no harm if I released him. But no sooner had I opened the cage than he tried to eat me. Do you think this is fair?'

'Fair! Course it's fair!' answered the old tree immediately. 'What do you human beings know about fairness? Tell me that? You come and rest in the shade of my branches in Summer, you take my fruit and make all the use of me you can. And in Winter you come with your axes and proceed to chop me up for firewood. Do you call that fair? Of course the tiger's right to want to eat you. I'd eat you myself if I wasn't a vegetarian.'

At these words the tiger who had been standing sulkily beside Astika became much more cheerful, and showed signs of getting ready for a meal.

'One moment,' said Astika holding up his hand. 'We haven't finished yet. There are three more judges to ask.'

Soon afterwards they came across a bullock standing in between the shafts of a huge cart which was loaded high with mango fruits and yams which his master had collected from the forest. The master himself was having a drink at the river.

'Good day, Master Bullock,' said Astika. 'I see you are having a busy day.'

It was some moments before the bullock could say anything; he was so busy swishing his tail to keep off the flies which were biting him mercilessly.

'Good day,' repeated Astika.

'Good day? What is there particularly good about today? It's exactly the same as any other day—Saturdays and Sundays included.'

This was a bad start, but Astika nevertheless went on to ask the bullock the same question he had asked the old banyan tree.

'Now do you think it's fair that he should eat me after as good as promising not to hurt me?' he asked when he had finished.

'Fair? Fair?' said the bullock. 'What's "fair" mean? Do you think it's fair that a bullock should be made to work like an elephant? Do you think it's fair that I should have to stand here in the hot sun while my master dips his head in the river? Do you think it's fair that we bullocks should be turned out to look after ourselves when we are too old to work. Fair? How dare a human being talk about fairness.' He turned to the tiger. 'For all I care you can eat him this moment. And you might like to eat my master as well. He'll be along in a minute.'

Astika hurriedly reminded the tiger that there were still two more judges to go.

They returned along the track they had come until they reached the small stretch of road leading to the village. The road was an old one, ill kept and pitted with holes. Its borders crumbled away into deep ditches which were filled with refuse and rotting leaves. And in a number of places weeds grew up between the cracks in its surface.

'I beg your pardon,' said Astika to the dusty old road. 'I'm sorry to disturb you, but we have a problem and were wondering if you would help us.'

'You have a problem?' creaked the road. 'That's a good one! Me help you! He! He! I'll crack my surface laughing. What about you helping me, eh? What about getting me a shovel of gravel to eat? Can't you see I'm wasting away?'

'I'm very sorry, but we haven't got any gravel. What we really came for was advice.'

'What is it then?' asked the road wearily.

And Astika repeated the story of the trouble between himself and the tiger, and asked the road to plead with the tiger for justice.

'Justice?' cackled the road. 'You want justice? Didn't you know? He's dead. Dead a long time! Look at me. I serve everyone, the rich, the poor, the honest and the dishonest. I help everyone who has need of my services. And what do I get in return? Nothing! No! That's not quite true. I do get something. I get rubbish thrown all over me. People spit on me. I am left to rot away in the sun and the dirt. There is no justice, my friend. The tiger wouldn't be natural if he showed any justice.'

At this the tiger could hardly control himself.

'Three out of four have agreed with me,' he insisted. 'Come now. You can't hope to escape. Give up, and let me eat you.'

At this very moment a fox came along. He was a large, red, furry fellow with a sharp eye.

'Hello,' he called, seeing Astika and the tiger deep in conversation, and guessing that the tiger was having an argument with his future dinner.

'What's all the argument about?'

'Dear friend,' said Astika quickly, 'I'm in terrible trouble and need your help.'

'You won't get any help from him,' sneered the tiger. 'The only one he ever helps is himself.'

'Let's hear what it's all about?' asked the fox, ignoring these rude remarks.

It was the tiger this time who explained what had happened. And when he had finished he ran his tongue impatiently round his lips and stood waiting to start his meal.

'What's your verdict?' he asked. 'Quick! I'm hungry. And I think it only honest to point out,' he added, 'that should it not be a favourable one I might find room for both a pilgrim and a fox in my stomach. So I'm sure your verdict will be a just one, won't it, Fox, old man?'

'Eh? Oh yes,' said Fox seeming absent-minded. 'By the way, I'm not quite sure I heard the beginning of the story correctly. Would you mind repeating it?'

Impatiently the tiger went over the beginning again. When he had finished however, Fox still looked very puzzled.

'Did you say you were in the cage, or the pilgrim was?' he asked.

'I said I was, you idiot!'

'I see! And you let him out?'

'No! No! Dolt. I said I was in the cage, and he let me out.'

'But how could he let you out of the cage if he was in it himself?'

'He wasn't in it,' shrieked the furious tiger. 'I was in it. Here, let me show you.' And he leapt into the cage which was on the other side of the road. 'I was in the cage and——' But his words were interrupted by the clanging noise made by the door as Fox quickly shut and bolted it. 'Hey! What the——? Stop it! Open the door—— Let me out—— It's not fair!'

At these last words Fox sniggered.

'I don't suppose it is. But it's a very wicked world, as you yourself said.' And with a polite good day to the tiger, and something like a wink to Astika, Fox turned away and strolled back into the forest.

By the time the crab had finished telling his story, Karla had recovered sufficiently from the effects of the snake bite to continue on his way. And he and the crab journeyed on together until they reached the lonely river the crab had told him about. And there, after many friendly exchanges and promises of future meetings, they sadly parted company.

2

Diplomacy

When they had heard these stories, Karataka said, 'I think we'd better go along and see the King now. He's like the Emperor, the carrion crow and the tiger all rolled into one. If we go, he'll wonder what new tricks we're up to, and if we don't go, he'll suspect we're hatching a plot against him and have us arrested.'

So the two Ministers bathed in a forest lake, and brushed their fur until it shone, and set out to meet the King.

It was easy to see that the King was worried from the deep creases in his forehead and the constant swishing of his tail. And the Ministers were not surprised when he took them quickly aside into his private rooms.

'Did you hear it?' he asked, as soon as they were alone.

'Hear what?' inquired Damanaka.

'Th—that terrible roaring in the forest.'

'We did hear something, Your Majesty.'

'Wasn't—wasn't it h-horrible?'

The Ministers glanced quickly at one another.

'It's a monster,' continued the King, before anyone could say anything. 'That's what it is. A monster! It has come to rob me of my throne. Did you ever hear any normal animal make such a terrible noise?'

'But, Your Majesty——'

'I tell you it's a monster.'

'Your Majesty,' said Karataka, who guessed that the monster was only a bull, 'there is no need for you to fear. No animal in the world is as strong as you are.'

'Animal, no. But this was a monster, not just an animal,' insisted the King, frightening himself more and more. 'He'll take away my throne—drive me into exile. I shall have to leave the country, go into foreign parts. I shall emigrate— that's what I shall do, emigrate to some distant land where they've never heard of monsters. Oh dear! Oh dear! At my age too.'

'If Your Majesty wishes,' said Karataka before the King could say any more, 'we shall investigate the matter. We will if you wish, go and seek this terrible creature and make a peace treaty with him.'

'Excellent idea. I mean, it was exactly what I was going to suggest myself.' And the two Ministers set out to look for the monster.

They had not gone very far before they discovered him grazing harmlessly by the roadside, not far from the ditch into which he had fallen. The pure water of the forest and the fresh grass had quickly restored him to health. And except for the fact that he was alone and nervous to be in a strange world, he was none the worse for his accident. The Ministers laughed to themselves at the thought that this was the terrible beast that their King was so worried about.

'Good morning,' said Karataka with a sweeping bow.

'Good morning, sir,' replied the simple-minded bull, greatly impressed by the fine glossy coats and courtly manners of the Ministers.

'You are a stranger in these parts, are you not?' asked Karataka.

'I am indeed,' replied the bull. 'To tell the truth, I'm a little frightened. You see, I've always lived in a village, and they tell me that there are—are wild animals like lions and elephants in these forests. Have you ever seen any?'

'We have seen one or two,' replied Karataka smiling. 'But they won't hurt you if you show them proper respect.'

'I wouldn't know how to,' said the bull. 'I'm country bred and don't know much about fine ways.'

'We'll teach you,' offered Karataka. 'Would you like to come with us to the court of the Lion-King?'

'The L-Lion-King,' repeated the bull, frightened by the 'Lion' part of the title.

'Oh, he won't hurt you. In fact he sent us as his messengers to greet you and invite you to come with us to his court.'

'You see,' added Damanaka, 'he has heard about you already and wishes to have the pleasure of speaking to you.'

'Does he really?'

'Yes. You are to be an honoured guest at the court of the King.'

And so the Ministers led the bull to the court, but left him waiting outside while they told the King of the great difficulties they had had in getting the mighty bull to agree to a peace treaty.

'Wh—what is he like?' asked the King.

'He's a powerful Bull King, Your Majesty.'

'Is—is he very fierce?'

'Oh yes,' replied Karataka, 'very fierce indeed.'

'W—will he attack me?'

'Ha! Ha! That was a very good joke, Your Majesty,' laughed Karataka. 'Who would dare to attack the great

Lion-King, the Scourge of the Forest? No indeed, Your Majesty. He has promised to meet you as a peaceful visiting king.'

'You have done very well,' said the King, reassured by these words. 'And as a reward I appoint you Grand Chief Minister to the Crown, and you Damanaka, Keeper of the Royal Bed-Straw.'

'Thank you, Your Majesty,' said both Ministers bowing humbly.

The meeting of the Lion and Bull Kings was a historic event. It was most dignified. As the bull entered the lion rose from his throne. Each stood for a moment admiring the other. The bull took a step forward. The lion took a step forward. The bull took another step forward. The lion did the same. And slowly, each approached nearer and nearer to the other with grave stately movements. Then they both bowed deeply, and embraced as friends. That, at least, was what it looked like to the members of the court. To Karataka and his friend, who could guess what was going on in the minds of the two, it looked very different. Despite all their wisdom and training in court manners, they had to turn away many times to hide their laughter. The truth was that the lion and the bull were terrified of one another. As the bull entered he glanced quickly at the huge lion with its wild mane, its large teeth and steely claws and instantly froze with fear. The lion, for his part seeing the powerful bull, its horns, great glittering spikes almost reaching the ceiling, stood awed and unable to move. It was fear of punishment that made the bull take the first step forward—although he very much wished it could have been in the opposite direction. Fear too made the lion come forward to meet the 'monster' whose bellows had made him think of fleeing the country.

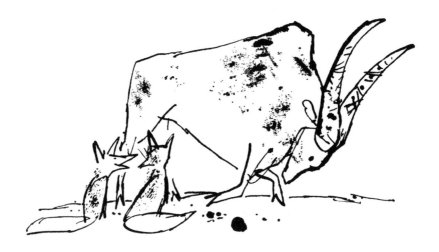

As they approached near to each other, the bull, in imitation of Karataka's greeting in the forest, gave a low, sweeping, and very clumsy bow. To the King it looked as if he were about to charge him. It was Karataka who saved the situation.

'See how gracefully he bows,' he said in a loud voice to his friend beside him.

Heartened by these words the King himself bowed, and both animals stood bowing to each other, their foreheads almost touching the ground, while the members of the court applauded loudly. It was over. The King and the bull were so relieved that neither was the monster the other believed him to be that they embraced and quickly became good friends. And within a week the King had found a room for the bull inside the palace and turned to the simple-minded bull for advice more often than to his Ministers.

The Ministers soon realized their mistake in bringing the bull to the palace. For all the notice the King took of them, now that he had a new friend, they might as well be banished again from the court.

'What are we to do?' asked Damanaka.

'We've been very short-sighted,' replied the other, 'rather like the wise man and the dishonest servant. Have you ever heard that story?'

'No,' replied Damanaka. 'What was it about?'

THE SAGE AND THE SERVANT

There once lived in the forest near the village of Kaveri in the South, a hermit by name of Deva Sarma. He had been a very rich man before becoming a hermit, and even when he gave up his home and his many servants, he still carried about a large sum of money which he put for safety in the hollow of the staff he used to help him in his travels.

Now the knowledge of this treasure reached the ears of a certain scoundrel living in the village, who immediately began to make plans to steal the hermit's money. But how was he to do it? Nobody, not even the worst of scoundrels dared to rob a hermitage or attack a Holy Man on his journeys. And anyway, our rogue was not this sort of thief. Anyone could rob a man walking along a lonely road at night. But not everybody could play a trick on so wise a person. This is how he did it.

One day he walked into the hermitage dressed in a simple white garment and with so serious an expression on his face that no one could doubt but that his mind was full of religious thoughts.

'What do you want, my son?' asked the hermit.

'Father,' came the reply, 'for a long time now I have watched you coming in and out of the village. I have stood by unseen in order just to catch a glimpse of you. I was a bad man, a dishonest man—one who had wicked thoughts about his fellow men. But ever since I first saw you I have changed.'

'I am pleased to hear it, my son,' said the hermit, flattered by these words. 'But why have you come here today?'

'To ask a favour,' was the reply. 'I have decided to become a hermit like you and wish to learn about a hermit's life. And so I have come to ask you if you will take me as your servant. In that way I can look after you, learn from you, and finally become a hermit myself. Will you take me as your servant?'

'My son,' said the hermit, 'I am happy to think that my example has turned you away from your evil ways. Stay with me for a while, and learn all you can. But do not consider yourself my servant. I myself am only a servant, a servant of God.

But the rogue preferred to be the servant of the hermit, having long ago given up the service of the Other Master. And he very quickly turned himself into the hermit's servant. He discovered which foods he most liked to eat, what stories he most enjoyed hearing, what music gave him most pleasure, and a number of other small, but important things to gain the trust of his master. And the hermit began to rely on him. He gave him his sacred books to keep for him, his religious robes, his sandal-wood burner, his stores of food, everything— everything that is, except the stick which contained the money.

This state of affairs did not please the self-appointed servant, however, for he held this prize above all others. And he set out to convince his master that he was the most honest servant anyone had ever employed.

'Master! Master!' he cried one day, running towards

the hermit, the tears streaming from his eyes and his face twisted with grief.

'What is it, my son?'

'Punish me, master! I deserve the most awful punishment.'

'Punish you? What for?'

'I am a thief!'

'What have you stolen?' asked the hermit more sternly.

'This!' he said, bringing out a straw from the back of his turban.

'How did you steal that?' asked his master, relieved that it was so small thing.

'When I was visiting some people in the village my head brushed against the top of the doorway and the straw must have fallen on to my turban. I am a thief, a miserable thief.'

'But you did not steal it purposely,' replied the hermit.

'Stealing is stealing,' said his servant. 'Whether it is done on purpose or otherwise. Punish me, master. Tell me what I must do to cleanse myself of this sin?'

'Go and bathe yourself three times in the river,' said the hermit, 'and this sin will be forgiven.'

The servant set out immediately to do as he was commanded. And from that moment the hermit gave him his entire trust.

One day the hermit and his servant set out on a pilgrimage to the sacred Ganges to seek forgiveness for all their sins. On the afternoon of the fourth day they arrived at a leisurely flowing river.

'Rest yourself, master,' said the servant. 'You have been travelling without rest since sunrise. Sit down beside the river and bathe your feet.'

Glad of the opportunity to rest, the hermit bathed his feet thankfully in the cool water.

'Why not have a bathe?' suggested the servant.

'I'd like that very much indeed,' replied his master. 'Stay here on the bank then and guard my clothes.' And he gave him everything he had—including the precious stick. Then he waded into the stream for his bathe.

The dishonest servant waited until he was well into the stream before picking up the hermit's treasure. He had succeeded at last. The money was his. So delighted was he at his own cleverness that he couldn't resist boasting of it to his victim.

'Look, old man,' he shouted to the hermit. 'A thief is stealing your money!' He held the precious stick firmly in his hand. 'Not just a straw this time, is it? I'll have to do a lot more penance for stealing this! Take a last look at your money, old miser. You'll never see it again. Take a last——'

But the sentence was never finished. At least it was not finished in the way that the rogue intended it to be. For instead he gave a horrible scream as a heavy something, smelling of the dead leaves of the forest, wound itself round his body. For a serpent, unseen by the thief as he stood boasting of his cleverness, had stolen up behind him. From the stream the helpless old man could only watch the struggle on the shore. There was nothing he could do.

It was a much wiser Wise Man who finally made his way home through the forest. And every day after that he said a prayer for the soul of the foolish man whom he had tempted to his death by carrying about so much money with him.

'It was indeed a stupid thing to do,' agreed Damanaka at the finish of the story. 'We have been stupid as well. But how can we get rid of our enemy?'

'That shouldn't be very difficult,' replied his friend.

'He is rather a big animal, though,' added Damanaka thoughtfully.

'All you need is a little cunning. You surely know the tale of the crow who took his revenge on the serpent?'

'No,' replied Damanaka. 'If it helps us in any way with our problem it might be worth hearing.'

THE CROW AND THE SERPENT

Once there lived in a corner of the forest a crow, who was a good, hardworking husband and who had never been known to say a harsh word to anyone. But at the time this story begins he had plenty of reason to use a great number of harsh and very angry words. For a serpent had found his nest and robbed it of all the eggs. Mrs. Crow was very upset indeed and begged her husband to leave the nest.

'It's no use staying here now that the serpent has found our nest,' she argued. 'What's to prevent his coming back next season and doing the same thing again? Let's leave this unhappy place.'

'This has been my home for as long as I can remember, and I'm not leaving it now,' replied her husband.

'But it's dangerous to stay. The serpent might return at any moment and kill us.'

'No,' said the crow firmly, 'I'm not going.' Then he added, 'I'll—I'll just have to—get rid of the serpent, that's all.'

'Don't be silly,' said his wife. 'How can you kill a serpent?'

'I'll think of a way.' And seeing how very upset she was, he told her the story of the hare that once killed a lion.

'A hare killing a lion?' laughed his wife. 'But a hare isn't strong enough.'

'He wasn't so foolish as to fight the lion. Listen to the story and you'll find out how he did it.'

THE LION AND THE HARE

There was once a ferocious lion who lived deep in the forest of Madunata where no human beings ever dared to go. It was a frightening place, all overgrown with sprawling branches and creepers and echoing the roars of savage animals. But most frightening of all was the lion himself who every day killed many deer, boars, buffaloes, wild goats, hares and countless other creatures. He hunted them not only because he wanted food, but also because he enjoyed doing it and was proud of his strength and savage skill.

Alarmed by this awful and unnecessary slaughter, the animals decided one day to try to come to an agreement with him.

'Your Majesty,' said a spokesman, addressing him by his title as King of the Beasts. 'We animals of the forest are very worried about all the destruction that has been going on. There is hardly anyone amongst us who has not lost a brother, a friend or some relation in the last few weeks. It's becoming so bad that we're frightened to leave our homes even to look for food, and are in danger of dying of starvation. Spare us, Your Majesty! Spare our lives and we shall send one of our number every day to your den and save you the trouble of having to hunt for your own food.'

The lion was very flattered by all this. He liked the idea of being waited upon by the animals of the forest.

'I agree to your plan,' he grunted. 'But make sure that the animal you send arrives promptly at midday and doesn't keep me waiting. Otherwise none of you will be left alive in the forest within a week.'

And so the agreement was reached, and every day after that one of their number was chosen by lot to go to the lion's den at midday.

One day the lot fell to a young hare. This creature didn't want to go any more than the others had. But unlike the others, he decided to do something about it. He thought and thought about it as he walked along to the lion's den.

'What shall I do? If I don't arrive at the den, my companions will all be killed within a week. Yet if I do, I shall be killed within an hour. What am I to do?'

As he walked along he noticed a well beside the track. He stopped for a few moments and stroked his chin thoughtfully.

'I wonder if—I wonder if——' But he never said aloud what it was that he wondered about. He continued his journey more hopefully than when he had started out.

When he finally arrived at the lion's den it was well past midday and the lion was pacing up and down in a fury.

'What's the meaning of this?' he roared.

'I'm—I'm sorry, Your Majesty,' said the hare, pausing at the door and looking nervously over his shoulder.

'I'm—I'm sorry I'm late, but——' He stopped and looked over his shoulder once more as if expecting something to attack him at any moment.

'Well, come in. I'm hungry! Hurry up!'

'Y-yes, Your Majesty,' stammered the hare, again looking nervously over his shoulder.

'What's the matter with you?' cried the lion, puzzled by his behaviour.

'It's—it's that lion, Your Majesty.'

'Lion? What lion, you fool?'

'The—the one I met on the way here. I had a terrible job getting away from him.'

'But didn't you tell him you were coming to my den?'

'Of course I did, but he only laughed.'

'He only what?' cried the outraged lion.

'He only laughed, Your Majesty. He said that he had no reason to be afraid of a lion who was too much of a coward to go out hunting animals himself, but expected them to come to his den. Those were his very words, Your Majesty.'

'Where is this—this upstart?' roared the lion.

'I'll take you to him, Your Majesty. I know the exact place where he lives.'

It was some time before the hare and the very impatient and angry lion got to the well.

'Where is he? Where is he?' demanded the lion when finally they arrived.

'He has taken fright at your coming and is hiding down this hole,' replied the hare.

The lion peered down into the well and saw his own reflection dimly outlined in the water below. He gave a great roar. The walls shook and the echo returned his cry like a challenging roar.

'Challenge me, does he?' shrieked the lion. 'We'll soon see which of us is the stronger.' And he leapt into the well to do battle with his enemy.

The hare waited only to hear the splash as he hit the water, before returning home.

'Where have you come from?'

'How did you get away?'

'Is—is the lion coming to kill us?'

110

The animals crowded round him, questioning him anxiously. He held up a paw.

'There's no need to worry about the lion any more,' he claimed. 'You see, I've killed him.'

Despite their fears, many animals laughed at these words.

'You've killed him, have you?'

'How did you do it?'

'Did you bite him?'

'What have you done with the body, eaten it?'

'Come with me,' he replied. And he took them to see the body in the well.

And ever afterwards the hare was highly regarded by all the animals of the forest. He became their teacher and was consulted on every important matter. And he never failed to give them good advice.

'That was a good story,' said Mrs. Crow laughing, when her husband had finished. And for a little while she forgot her fears of the serpent. But they returned very quickly when she saw her husband prepare to fly away to get their food.

'You won't be home late tonight, will you, dear?' she asked nervously.

'I won't,' he promised. 'Keep cheerful. Soon there'll be nothing to worry about at all.'

But he was by no means as happy as he wished his wife to believe. How did one kill a serpent? After all, it's no small task to expect of a creature whose only weapon is a not very sharp beak. And so that afternoon he decided to visit a friend and ask his advice.

His friend was Fox. They had known each other since childhood and often met together in the forest to have a chat.

'What's the matter?' asked Fox, seeing the unhappy look on his friend's face.

'A serpent's been raiding my nest and has taken all the eggs,' replied Crow. 'My wife wants us to go and live somewhere else.'

Fox shook his head sadly.

'What am I to do?' continued Crow. 'I don't want to go away, but it's dangerous to stay where we are.'

'It's a bad business,' agreed Fox. But after thinking for a while he added. 'I think I can help you. Now listen carefully to what I say and do everything exactly as I tell you.' And he outlined his plan to get rid of their enemy.

It happened that a Royal Princess used to come every day to bathe in a little pool not very far away from the tree in which Crow lived. She came with a few special friends, leaving the Guard of Honour stationed on the other side of the trees while they bathed. They made a charming, laughing, splashing picture as they played together in the water.

'Ooh, you're splashing me.'

'Take that.'

'You missed me. Ooh! Your Highness!'

'Caught you that time.'

'My hair! Look what you've done to my hair.'

'You should have worn a—— Look!' The Princess pointed to a large, black crow which was flying backwards and forwards very low over the water.

'I've never seen a crow behaving like that before.'

'I wonder if it's a man changed into a bird,' said one of the Princess's friends.

'Or a magician?' said another.

Frightened by their own words they hurried quickly into the deepest water they could find.

As soon as they were all away from the bank the crow landed beside the pile of clothes and ornaments belonging to the Princess and her friends. Then he calmly picked up a large necklace and flew away with it in his beak.

'Stop him! Stop thief!' cried the maids hurrying to get their clothes. 'Stop him! Guards! Guards!'

What a lot of noise they made as they ran after the crow!

'There he is! Over there! No! Here he comes.'

'Look! He's dropped the necklace into the hole over there by that tree.'

The guards quickly arrived at the hole, and with their swords began prodding about in it looking for the necklace. The serpent who lived in the hole, suddenly put his head out to see what was happening. The maids screamed. There was a loud command from the Officer of the Guards, then came a swift blow from a cudgel. And the serpent lay dead on the ground.

Crow and his wife watched all this from a branch in the tree above. When it was over they returned happily to their nest.

'We won't have to leave our home, after all,' Crow said joyfully, patting into place one or two loose twigs.

'No,' replied his wife, her fears now at rest. 'And we'll have to start getting ready for a new family very soon.'

'We'll have to ask Fox to be their godfather,' added Crow.

Damanaka smiled when his friend reached the end of the stories.

'It's funny how one story reminds you of another,' he said. 'I heard one some time ago which is rather like those you have just told me. Would you like to hear it?'

'Of course,' replied Karataka. 'I'm very fond of stories. Life wouldn't be worth much without them.'

114

THE LION AND THE GOAT

Once there was a goat, who because he had injured his leg and was unable to keep up with the herd, found himself one day left far behind the others and alone in the forest. And wishing to shelter from the heat of the sun and the attentions of wild animals, he decided to hide himself in a cave. It was very dark inside, and not until he had gone some way into it did he realize that there was another animal already there.

'Who's there?' he called, hoping that the animal was friendly. His call was answered by a grunt and a throaty roar, sounds which proclaimed their owner to be a lion.

'I didn't ask you to growl at me,' cried the goat, pretending to be angry. 'I only asked you who you were.'

Astonished at these brave words, the lion came out of the shadows to have a look at the intruder. When he saw that it was only a goat he growled once more and said gruffly, 'Those are brave words for a goat. What are you doing in my cave? Are you in a hurry to die?'

The goat, however, showed no fear.

'I really don't know how to put it,' he replied. 'It's rather a delicate matter.'

'A delicate matter,' repeated the lion, 'what is?'

'My being here. You see——'

'Out with it,' said the lion. 'Be quick! I'm feeling like a snack. You've come along just in time.'

'That does make it difficult,' continued the goat unmoved. 'You see, to tell the truth, I came here looking for you.'

'For me?' asked the lion. 'What do you want me for?'

'To kill you, I'm afraid.'

'T—to kill me?'

'I'm really very sorry. It's such an awful nuisance. It's the herd, you know. They insist.'

'The—the herd insist?' repeated the lion bewildered, and becoming a little afraid in spite of himself.

'Perhaps I'd better explain,' continued the goat. 'As King of the Goats——' Here he gave a little bow as if introducing himself, 'every now and again I have a duty to perform—a rather unpleasant one I'm afraid. I've got to prove to my people that I'm still as strong as ever. It's rather silly, really. Everyone knows how strong I am. But—well, you understand. Some people are never satisfied.'

'Wh—what have you got to do?' asked the lion.

'Nothing much—just a few tigers—and the odd elephant.'

'T—tigers and e-elephants. What do you do with them?'

'Oh, kill them,' replied the goat casually. 'It's all a bit messy.'

'B—but what do you want with me? I'm not a tiger or an elephant.'

'The wife, as a matter of fact.'

'The wife?'

'Yes, it's really nothing to do with the other business. You see, she's getting a bit fed up with all those elephant hides and tiger skins around the place. She wants a lion skin for a change. It's all a bit silly. But you know what women are.'

The lion began to move towards the opening of the cave.

'Are you going somewhere?' asked the goat.

'Y—yes. You heard me cough when you came in. I—I've got a cold. My throat's been a bit sore lately. I—I'm just off down the river for a drink. Shan't be long.' And he ran quickly out of the cave.

He had not gone very far when he bumped into a fox.

116

'S—sorry. I—I can't stay. I'm being hunted by the King of the Goats,' he said. And he hurried on.

The fox ran after him.

'What?' he laughed. 'You, running away from a goat?'

'It's the King of the Goats,' explained the lion. 'He's already killed a lot of tigers and—and the odd elephant. I really can't stop.'

'Wait a moment. This sounds like a trick to me,' said the fox.

'Firstly, there is no King of the Goats, not at least that I know of. And secondly, no goat ever killed a single tiger, let alone the odd elephant. Someone's making a fool of you.'

The lion stopped. 'Do you really think—— Of course! I wasn't really taken in by him. I—I was only running down to the river for a drink. I've got a cold—and a very sore throat.'

'The river's not this way,' said the fox smiling.

'No, how silly of me. I really can't think clearly when I've got a cold.'

'Er—shall we go back and make a meal of this trickster?' asked the fox.

'That's exactly what I was going to do,' replied the lion. 'You know, I never really thought he was the King of the Goats. You can't fool me as easily as that.'

And so the fox and the lion returned to the cave where the goat had settled himself comfortably on the bed of rushes left by the lion, and was munching some tender grass shoots he had brought with him. When he saw the fox come in with the lion he guessed what had happened.

'You know, Fox, old man, this really won't do,' he said before anyone else could say a word.

'What do you mean?' asked the fox puzzled. 'What won't do?'

'You haven't carried out my instructions properly.'

'Your instructions?'

'Yes. I particularly asked you to fetch me a handsome young lion with a fine glossy coat. This fellow you've brought is much too old to make a good hearth rug. Really! I've a good mind to give you a beating for this.'

At these words the lion, thinking he had been betrayed by the fox turned to him growling fiercely. Seeing it was no use arguing with the enraged lion he darted out of the cave, closely followed by the lion.

Idly the goat watched them go. Taking his time he finished the last of the sweet, delicious grasses he was munching. It was now almost dark and a safe time to return home. And helping himself to one or two useful bits of food left by the lion, he ambled slowly out of the cave.

3

Conclusion

'That was an excellent trick,' said Karataka at the end of the story. 'That's just the sort of thing we want to do. Our master's very much like the lion in that story.'

'He's certainly as foolish,' agreed his friend. 'It'd be hard to say which was the more stupid. Do you remember the time he sent a messenger up a pine tree to get a pineapple?'

The two Ministers laughed uproariously at this. In fact, so busy were they laughing and sneering that they didn't notice the lion, their master, standing close behind them listening to their conversation.

'He'd believe anything we told him,' said Karataka gaily. 'He's just a big fool. Listen! I've just had an idea. I think I know how we can get rid of that stupid bull—and we'll make the King himself do it.' And he gave the details of his plan to rid themselves of their rival at court.

That afternoon the Ministers were alone with the King in the royal cave. It had been a dark overcast day and the rain was falling steadily.

'You two are looking very thoughtful,' said the King. 'What's worrying you?'

'N—nothing, Your Majesty,' replied Karataka.

'What do you mean "n—nothing"?' asked the King. 'Why not just plain "nothing"?'

'It's n—nothing—really, Your Majesty.'

'Now it's "n—nothing—really". This sounds bad. There is something, and you're keeping it from me. What is it?'

'It's—it's——'

'Stop stuttering,' ordered the King. 'If it's important, tell me.'

'It—it would only make you angry.'

'Tell me this instant,' demanded the King impatiently.

The Ministers looked at each other sorrowfully.

'We will obey, Your Majesty,' said Karataka.

'Now, what is it?'

'It's very secret.'

'Get on with it.'

'Your friend the bull is—is planning a—a revolution.'

'A revolution!' roared the lion.

'We—we thought it our duty to tell you.'

'How is he going to do it?'

'Later this afternoon he is coming to this very cave to assassinate you.'

'Is he indeed?' snarled the Lion-King. 'Well, he can come when he likes. I shan't run away from him.'

By now the rain was falling very heavily indeed. Clouds

almost blackened the afternoon sky and there was thunder in the distance. From inside the cave the animals watched the flashes of far-away lightning and were thankful to be in so good a shelter. Then suddenly they noticed something on the horizon. At first it appeared only as a speck on the hillside. Then as it came nearer they made it out to be the shape of an animal, a large animal. As it came still nearer, they recognized it as the bull. He was hurrying towards the cave to shelter from the storm.

'Your Majesty, Your Majesty,' said Karataka, drawing the King's attention to the charging beast. 'It's your rival the bull. He is coming to assassinate you.'

And indeed to the King and his Ministers, the bull appeared wild with rage as he lashed furiously with his tail and whirled his head to shake off the rain.

'He's coming to assassinate me, is he?' cried the lion. 'We'll soon see about that.'

And without another word he charged out of the cave to meet his enemy. The Ministers smiled at one another and went outside to enjoy the fun.

Everything in between the charging animals, shrubs, dead leaves, twigs, stones were swept out of their way. Heads forward, tails high, their large bodies surged forward. Nearer and nearer they came, closer and closer. The Ministers stood tensed with excitement. Closer and closer they came. They had almost reached one another. Closer! Closer! Then —they stopped. They stopped and stood facing one another. There were no growls, no ragings, no slashing with claw or horn. They just stopped. For a moment nothing happened. Then they both turned slowly. And side by side they marched purposefully back towards the cave where the two Ministers were standing.

Karataka was quick to realize what had happened.

'I—wonder why they're coming towards us,' said Damanaka.

'We'd better not wait to find out,' replied his friend.

The two animals turned tail and dashed towards the forest. The lion and the bull followed. They crossed the plain. The lion and the bull followed. They clambered over the hills. The lion and the bull followed. Then they came to a wide river.

'I can't swim very well,' said Damanaka.

'It's surprising how quickly one can learn,' replied his friend as they leapt in.

The lion and the bull arrived shortly afterwards at the bank and watched the Ministers as they struck out for the opposite shore.

'That's the last of them,' said the lion.

'I think you'll be better off without them,' commented the bull as they turned for home.

That evening at the palace, the lion said the last word about the banished Ministers. 'The trouble with them,' he yawned, just before he fell asleep, 'is that they listen to too many stories.'